GW00986164

THE ASUTRA

As Anome, Etzwane of necessity had avoided notoriety; he was not a conspicuous man in any event. He moved with economy, spoke in a flat voice, used no gesticulations, all of which made for a sombre force disproportionate to his years. When Etzwane looked in a mirror he often felt a discord between his image, which was saturnine, even a trifle grim, and what he felt to be his true self: a being beset by doubts, shivered by passions, jerked here and there by irrational exhilarations; a person oversusceptible to charm and beauty, wistful with longing for the unattainable. So Etzwane half-seriously regarded himself. Only when he played music did he feel a convergence of his incongruous parts.

Then came the Asutra.

Also by the same author,
and available in Coronet Books:

The Anome
The Brave Free Men
The Gray Prince
Big Planet
Showboat World

The Asutra

Durdane Book 3

Jack Vance

CORONET BOOKS
Hodder and Stoughton

Copyright © 1973 Jack Vance

First published in Great Britain by
Coronet Books 1975

Second impression 1977

The characters and situations in this book are entirely imaginary and bear no relation to any real person or actual happening.

This book is sold subject to the condition that it shall not, by way of trade or otherwise, be lent, re-sold, hired out or otherwise circulated without the publisher's prior consent in any form of binding or cover other than that in which this is published and without a similar condition including this condition being imposed on the subsequent purchaser.

Printed and bound in Great Britain for
Hodder and Stoughton Paperbacks, a
division of Hodder and Stoughton Ltd.,
Mill Road, Dunton Green, Sevenoaks,
Kent (Editorial Office: 47 Bedford
Square, London, WC1 3DP) by
Hunt Barnard Printing Ltd.,
Aylesbury, Bucks.

ISBN 0 340 19830 3

FLANDRY OF TERRA

POUL ANDERSON

Captain Sir Dominic Flandry was a top man in the Intelligence Corps of the Imperial Terrestrial Navy. He knew that on the outer edges of the empire, civilization was spread hideously thin. The stars faded towards barbarism, with the great evil Empire of Merseia beyond.

But there were times when Flandry abandoned his senior position of command to go out in the field. Then he operated like the cool and brilliant agent he was, a ruthless, highly-trained professional. And in these three fast-moving adventures Captain Dominic Flandry shows that a space-age secret agent *has* to stay on top of the job – or succumb to nameless horrors.

CORONET BOOKS

ALSO AVAILABLE IN CORONET BOOKS

	JACK VANCE	
☐ 19827 3	The Anome	75p
☐ 19827 3	The Brave Free Men	75p
☐ 20820 1	The Gray Prince	60p
☐ 21251 9	Big Planet	65p
☐ 21252 7	Showboat World	65p
	RICHARD AVERY	
	The Expendables:	
☐ 19472 3	The Deathworms Of Kratos	35p
☐ 19889 3	The Rings Of Tantalus	40p
☐ 19875 3	The War Games Of Zelos	50p
☐ 19918 0	Venom Of Argus	60p
	POUL ANDERSON	
☐ 16337 2	Beyond The Beyond	35p
☐ 16336 4	Tau Zero	35p
☐ 18615 1	The Byworlder	35p
☐ 19864 8	Ensign Flandry	65p
☐ 20753 1	Flandry Of Terra	70p
☐ 21245 4	Agent Of The Terran Empire	70p
	PHILIP K. DICK	
☐ 21829 0	The Turning Wheel and Other Stories	80p
☐ 21830 4	Counter-Clock World	70p

All these books are available at your local bookshop or newsagent, or can be ordered direct from the publisher. Just tick the titles you want and fill in the form below.

Prices and availability subject to change without notice.

CORONET BOOKS, P.O. Box 11, Falmouth, Cornwall.

Please send cheque or postal order, and allow the following for postage and packing:

U.K. – One book 22p plus 10p per copy for each additional book ordered, up to a maximum of 82p.

B.F.P.O. and EIRE–22p for the first book plus 10p per copy for the next 6 books, thereafter 4p per book.

OTHER OVERSEAS CUSTOMERS – 30p for the first book and 10p per copy for each additional book.

Name ....

Address ....

....

Chapter 1

The Roguskhoi and their dominant asutra had been expelled from Shant. Belabored on the ground by the Brave Free Men, tormented from above by the Flyers of Shant, the Roguskhoi had retreated south, across the Great Salt Bog into Palasedra. In a dismal valley the horde had been destroyed, with only a handful of chieftains escaping in a remarkable red-bronze spaceship – and so the strange invasion of Shant had come to an end.

For Gastel Etzwane the victory brought a temporary joy after which he fell into a dour and introspective mood. He became aware of a vast aversion to responsibility, to public activity in general; he marveled that he had functioned as well and as long as he had. Returning to Garwiy he took himself from the Council of Purple Men with almost offensive abruptness; he became Gastel Etzwane the musician: so much, no more. At once his spirits soared; he felt free and whole. Two days the mood persisted, then waned as the question *What now?* found no natural or easy response.

On a hazy autumn morning, with the three suns lazing behind self-generated disks of milk-white, pink, and blue nimbus, Etzwane walked along Galias Avenue. Tape trees trailed purple and gray ribbons about his head; beside him moved the Jardeen River on its way to the Sualle. Other folk strolled along Galias Avenue, but none took notice of the man who so recently had ruled their lives. As Anome, Etzwane of necessity had avoided notoriety; he was not a conspicuous man in any event. He moved with economy, spoke in a flat voice, used no gesticulations, all of which made for a somber force disproportionate to his years. When Etzwane looked in a mirror he often felt a discord between his image, which was saturnine, even a trifle grim, and what he felt to be his true self: a being beset by doubts, shivered by passions, jerked here and there by irrational exhilarations; a person oversusceptible to charm and beauty, wistful with longing for the unattainable. So Etzwane half-seriously regarded himself. Only when he played music did he feel a convergence of his incongruous parts.

What now?

He had long taken the answer for granted: he would rejoin Frolitz and the Pink-Black-Azure-Deep Greeners. Now he was not so sure, and he halted to watch broken strands from the tape trees drifting along the river. The old music sounded in his mind far away, a wind blowing out of his youth.

He turned away from the river and continued along the avenue, and presently came upon a three-storied structure of black and gray-green glass with heavy mulberry lenses bulging over the street: Fontenay's Inn, which put Etzwane in mind of Ifness, Earthman and Research Fellow of the Historical Institute. After the destruction of the Roguskhoi he and Ifness had flown by balloon across Shant to Garwiy. Ifness carried a bottle containing an asutra taken from the corpse of a Roguskhoi chieftain. The creature resembled a large insect, eight inches long and four inches in thickness: a hybrid of ant and tarantula, mingled with something unimaginable. Six arms, each terminating in three clever palps, depended from the torso. At one end ridges of purple-brown chitin protected the optical process: three oil-black balls in shallow cavities tufted with hair. Below trembled feeder mechanisms and a cluster of mandibles. During the journey Ifness occasionally tapped on the glass, to which the asutra returned only a flicker of the optical organs. Etzwane found the scrutiny unnerving; somewhere within the glossy torso subtle processes were occurring: ratiocination, or an equivalent operation; hate, or a sensation analogous.

Ifness refused to speculate upon the nature of the asutra. 'Guesses are of no value. The facts, as we know them, are ambiguous.'

'The asutra tried to destroy the folk of Shant,' declared Etzwane. 'Is this not significant?'

Ifness only shrugged and looked out across the purple distances of Canton Shade. They now sailed close-hauled into a north wind, bucking and sliding as the winch-tender coaxed the best from the *Conseil*, a notoriously cranky balloon.

Etzwane attempted another question. 'You examined the asutra you took from Sajarano: what did you learn?'

Ifness spoke in a measured voice. 'The asutra metabolism is unusual and beyond the scope of my analysis. They seem a congenitally parasitical form of life, to judge from the feeding apparatus. I have discovered no disposition to communicate, or perhaps the creatures use a method too subtle for my comprehension. They enjoy the use of paper and pencil and make neat geometrical patterns, sometimes of considerable complication but no obvious meaning. They show ingenuity in solving problems and appear to be both patient and methodical.'

'How did you learn all this?' demanded Etzwane.

'I devised tests. It is all a matter of presenting inducements.'

'Such as?'

'The possibility of freedom. The avoidance of discomfort.'

Etzwane, faintly disgusted, mulled the matter over for a period. Presently he asked, 'What do you intend to do now? Will you return to Earth?'

Ifness looked up into the lavender sky, as if taking note of some far destination. 'I hope to continue my inquiries; I have much to gain and little to lose. With equal certainty I will encounter official discouragement. My nominal superior, Dasconetta, has nothing to gain and much to lose.'

Curious, thought Etzwane; was this the way things went on Earth? The Historical Institute imposed a rigorous discipline upon its Fellows, enjoying absolute detachment from the affairs of the world under examination. So much he knew of Ifness, his background, and his work. Little enough, everything considered.

The journey proceeded. Ifness read from *The Kingdoms of Old Caraz*; Etzwane maintained a half-resentful silence. The *Conseil* spun up the slot; cantons Erevan, Maiy, Conduce, Jardeen, Wild Rose passed below and disappeared into the autumn murk. The Jardeen Gap opened ahead; the Ushkadel rose to either side; the *Conseil* blew along the Vale of Silence, through the gap, and so to South Station under the astounding towers of Garwiy.

The station gang hauled the *Conseil* down to the platform; Ifness alighted, and with a polite nod for Etzwane set off across the plaza.

In a sardonic fury Etzwane watched the spare figure disappear into the crowd. Ifness clearly meant to avoid even the most casual of relationships. Now, two days later, looking across Galias Avenue, Etzwane was once again reminded of Ifness. He crossed the avenue and entered Fontenay's Inn.

The day-room was quiet; a few figures sat here and there in the shadows musing over their mugs. Etzwane went to the counter, where he was attended by Fontenay himself. 'Well then: it's Etzwane the musician! If you and your khitan are seeking a place, it can't be done. Master Hesselrode and his Scarlet-Mauve-Whiters work the stand. No offense intended; you scratch with the best of them. Accept a mug of Wild Rose ale, at no charge.'

Etzwane raised the mug. 'My best regards.' He drank. The old life had not been so bad after all. He looked around the chamber. There: the low platform where so often he had played music; the table where he had met lovely Jurjin of Xhiallinen; the nook where Ifness had waited for the Faceless Man. In every quarter hung memories which now seemed unreal; the world had become sane and ordinary . . . Etzwane peered across the room. In the far corner a tall, white-haired man of uncertain age sat making entries into a notebook. Mulberry light from a high bull's-eye played around him; as Etzwane watched, the man raised a goblet to his lips and sipped. Etzwane turned to Fontenay. 'The man in the far alcove – what of him?'

Fontenay glanced across the room. 'Isn't that the gentleman Ifness? He uses my front suite. An odd type, stern and solitary, but his money is as downright as sweat. He's from Canton Cape, or so I gather.'

'I believe I know the gentleman.' Etzwane took his mug and walked across the chamber. Ifness noted his approach sidewise, from the corner of his eye. Deliberately he closed his notebook and sipped from his goblet of ice water. Etzwane gave a polite salute and seated himself; had he waited for an invitation, Ifness might well have kept him standing. 'On impulse I stepped in, to recall our adventures together,' said Etzwane, 'and I find you engaged at the same occupation.'

Ifness' lips twitched. 'Sentimentality has misled you. I am here because convenient lodging is available and because I can work, usually without interruption. What of you? Have you no official duties to occupy you?'

'None whatever,' said Etzwane. 'I have resigned my connection with the Purple Men.'

'You have earned your liberty,' said Ifness in a nasal monotone. 'I wish you the pleasure of it. And now' – With meaningful exactitude he arranged his notebook.

'I am not reconciled to idleness,' said Etzwane. 'It occurs to me that I might be able to work with you.'

Ifness arched his eyebrows. 'I am not sure that I understand your proposal.'

'It is simple enough,' said Etzwane. 'You are a Fellow of the Historical Institute; you perform research on Durdane and elsewhere; you could use my assistance. We have worked together before; why should we not continue to do so?'

Ifness spoke in a crisp voice. 'The concept is impractical. My work for the most part is solitary, and occasionally takes me off-planet, which of course –'

Etzwane held up his hand. 'This is precisely my goal,' he declared, though the idea had never formed itself in terms quite so concrete. 'I know Shant well; I have traveled Palasedra; Caraz is a wilderness; I am anxious to visit other worlds.'

'These are natural and normal yearnings,' said Ifness. 'Nevertheless, you must make other arrangements.'

Etzwane pensively drank ale. Ifness watched stonily sidewise. Etzwane asked, 'You still study the asutra?'

'I do.'

'You feel that they have not yet done with Shant?'

'I am convinced of nothing.' Ifness spoke in his didactic monotone. 'The asutra tested a biological weapon against the men of Shant. The weapon – which is to say, the

Roguskhoi – failed because of crudities in execution, but no doubt served its purpose; the asutra are now better informed. Their options are still numerous. They can continue their experiments, using different weapons. On the other hand they may decide to expunge the human presence on Durdane altogether.'

Etzwane had no comment to make. He drained his mug and in spite of Ifness' disapprobation signaled Fontenay for replenishment. 'You are still trying to communicate with the asutra?'

'They are all dead.'

'And you made no progress?'

'Essentially none.'

'Do you plan to capture others?'

Ifness gave him a cool smile. 'My goals are more modest than you suspect. I am concerned principally for my status in the Institute, that I may enjoy my accustomed perquisites. Your interests and mine engage at very few points.'

Etzwane scowled and drummed his fingers on the table. 'You prefer that the asutra do not destroy Durdane?'

'As an abstract ideal I will embrace this proposition.'

'The situation itself is not abstract,' Etzwane pointed out. 'The Roguskhoi have killed thousands! If they won here they might go on to attack the Earth worlds.'

'The thesis is somewhat broad,' said Ifness. 'I have put it forward as a possibility. My associates, however, incline to other views.'

'How can there be doubt?' Etzwane demanded. 'The Roguskhoi are or were an aggressive force.'

'So it would seem, but against whom? The Earth worlds? Ridiculous; how could they avail against civilised weaponry?' Ifness made an abrupt gesture. 'Now please excuse me; a certain Dasconetta asserts his status at my expense, and I must consider the matter. It was pleasant to have seen you . . .'

Etzwane leaned forward. 'Have you identified the asutra home-world?'

Ifness gave his head an impatient shake. 'It might be one of twenty thousand, probably off towards the center of the galaxy.'

'Should we not seek out this world, to study it at close hand?'

'Yes, yes; of course.' Ifness opened his journal.

Etzwane rose to his feet. 'I wish you success in your struggle for status.'

'Thank you.'

Etzwane returned across the room. He drank another mug of ale, glowering back towards Ifness, who serenely sipped ice water and made notes in his journal.

Etzwane left Fontenay's Inn and continued north beside the Jardeen, pondering a possibility which Ifness himself might not have considered . . . He turned aside into the Avenue of Purple Gorgons, where he caught a diligence to the Corporation Plaza. He alighted at the Jurisdictionary and climbed to the offices of the Intelligence Agency on the second floor. The director was Aun Sharah, a handsome man, subtle and soft-spoken, with an Aesthete's penchant for casual elegance. Today he wore a suave robe of gray over a midnight blue body-suit; a star sapphire dangled from his left ear by a silver chain. He greeted Etzwane affably but with a wary deference that reflected their previous differences. 'I understand that you are once again an ordinary citizen,' said Aun Sharah. 'The metamorphosis was swift. Has it been complete?'

'Absolutely; I am a different person,' said Etzwane. 'When I think over the past year I wonder at myself.'

'You have surprised many folk,' said Aun Sharah in a dry voice. 'Including myself.' He leaned back in his chair.

'What now? Is it to be music once more?'

'Not just yet. I am unsettled and restless, and I am now interested in Caraz.'

'The subject is large,' said Aun Sharah in his easy, half-facetious manner. 'However, your lifetime lies before you.'

'My interest is not all-embracing,' said Etzwane. 'I merely wonder if Roguskhoi have ever been seen in Caraz.'

Aun Sharah gazed reflectively at Etzwane. 'Your term as private citizen has quickly run its course.'

Etzwane ignored the remark. 'Here are my thoughts. The Roguskhoi were tested in Shant and defeated. So much we know. But what of Caraz? Perhaps they were originally deployed in Caraz; perhaps a new horde is in formation. A dozen possibilities suggest themselves, including the chance that nothing whatever has happened.'

'True,' said Aun Sharah. 'Our intelligence is essentially local. Still, on the other hand, what can we do? We strain to encompass the work already required of us.'

'In Caraz news drifts down the rivers. At the seaports mariners learn of events occurring far inland. What if you circulated your men along the docks and through the waterfront taverns, to find what might be the news from Caraz?'

'The idea has value,' said Aun Sharah. 'I will issue such an order. Three days should suffice, at least for a preliminary survey.'

Chapter 2

The thin, dark, solitary boy who had taken to himself the name of Gastel Etzwane* had become a hollow-cheeked young man with an intense and luminous gaze. When Etzwane played music the corners of his mouth rose to bring a poetic melancholy to his otherwise saturnine features; otherwise his demeanor was quiet and controlled beyond the ordinary. Etzwane had no intimates save perhaps old Frolitz the musician, who thought him mad . . .

On the day following his visit to the Jurisdictionary he received a message from Aun Sharah. 'The investigation has yielded immediate information, in which I am sure you will be interested. Please call at your convenience.'

Etzwane went at once to the Jurisdictionary.

Aun Sharah took him to a chamber high in one of the sixth-level cupolas. Four-foot-thick sky lenses of water-green glass softened the lavender sunlight and intensified the colors of the Canton Glirris rug. The room contained a single table twenty feet in diameter, supporting a massive contour map. Approaching, Etzwane saw a surprisingly detailed representation of Caraz. Mountains were carved from pale Canton Faible amber, with inlaid quartz

* Among the Chilites of Temple Bashon, each Pure Boy selected for himself a name exemplifying his hopes for the future. Gastel was an heroic flyer of ancient times, Etzwane a legendary musician. The name had caused Etzwane's soul-father, Osso, shock and dissatisfaction.

to indicate the presence of snow and ice. Silver threads and ribbons indicated the rivers; the plains were gray-purple slate; cloth in various textures and colors represented forests and swamps. Shant and Palasedra appeared as incidental islands off the eastern flank.

Aun Sharah walked slowly along the northern edge of the table. 'Last night,' he said, 'a local Discriminator* brought in a seaman from the Gyrmont docks. He told a strange tale indeed, which he had heard from a bargeman at Erbol, here at the mouth of the Keba River.' Aun Sharah put his finger down on the map. 'The bargeman had floated a load of sulfur down from this area up here' – Aun Sharah touched a spot two thousand miles inland – 'which is known as Burnoun. About here is a settlement, Shillinsk; it is not shown . . . At Shillinsk the bargeman spoke to nomad traders from the west, beyond these mountains, the Kuzi Kaza . . .'

Etzwane returned to Fontenay's Inn in a diligence, to meet Ifness on his way out the door. Ifness gave him a distant nod and would have gone his way had not Etzwane stepped in front of him. 'A single moment of your time.'

Ifness paused, frowning. 'What do you require?'

'You mentioned a certain Dasconetta. He would be a person of authority?'

Ifness looked at Etzwane sidelong. 'He occupies a responsible post, yes.'

'How can I get in touch with Dasconetta?'

Ifness reflected. 'In theory, several methods exist. Practically, you would be forced to work through me.'

'Very well; be so good as to put me into contact with

* Discriminator: in the language of Shant, *avistioi* – literally, 'nice discriminator'. The *avistioi* originally were inspectors hired by the Garwiy Aesthetes, and only gradually assumed the function of the cantonal police. Etzwane and Aun Sharah had expanded their scope.

Dasconetta.'

Ifness gave a wintry chuckle. 'Matters are not all that simple. I suggest that you prepare a brief exposition of your business. You will submit this to me. In due course I will be in contact with Dasconetta, at which time I may be able to transmit your message, assuming, naturally, that I find it neither tendentious nor trivial.'

'All very well,' said Etzwane, 'but the matter is urgent. He will be sure to complain at any delay.'

Ifness spoke in a measured voice. 'I doubt if you are capable of predicting Dasconetta's reactions. The man makes a fad of unpredictability.'

'Nevertheless, I believe that he will give serious regard to my business,' said Etzwane, 'especially if he is concerned for his prestige. Is there no way to communicate with him directly?'

Ifness made a gesture of weary resignation. 'Well then, briefly, what is your proposal? If the matter is important, I can at least advise you.'

'I realise this,' said Etzwane. 'But you are preoccupied with research; you stated that you could not cooperate with me, that you lacked authority, and you implied that all must be referred to Dasconetta. Hence, the rational course is to discuss my business with Dasconetta at once.'

'You have misinterpreted my remarks,' said Ifness, his voice rising a trifle. 'I stated that I had no place for you in my entourage, that I could not escort you on a tour of the Earth worlds. I did not indicate that my authority was insufficient or that I deferred to Dasconetta in any respect, save that imposed by an administrative technicality. I must listen to your business, since this is my function. So then, what is the matter which has so excited you?'

Etzwane spoke tonelessly. 'A report out of Caraz has come to my attention. It may be no more than a rumor, but I feel that it must be investigated. To this end I need a swift vehicle, which I am sure Dasconetta can supply.'

'Aha! Well, well, indeed. And what is the nature of this rumor?'

Etzwane went on in a flat voice. 'Roguskhoi have appeared in Caraz: a considerable horde.'

Ifness gave a curt nod. 'Go on.'

'The horde fought an army of men, who reputedly used energy weapons. The Roguskhoi were apparently defeated, but here the rumor is uncertain.'

'What is the source of this information?'

'A mariner who heard the tale from a Caraz bargeman.'

'Where did the occurrence take place?'

'Is not this irrelevant?' asked Etzwane. 'I am requesting only a suitable vehicle in which to investigate the business.'

Ifness spoke gently, as if to an irrational child. 'The situation is more complex than you suppose. If you communicated this request to Dasconetta, or anyone else of the Coordination, they would merely refer the matter back to me, with a sharp comment as to my competence. Further, you know the proscriptions which control Fellows of the Institute: we never interfere with the flow of local events. I have violated this precept, of course, but so far I have been able to justify my acts. If I allowed you to place this remarkable request before Dasconetta, they would think me not only irresponsible but foolish. There is no help for it. I agree that the rumor is significant, and whatever my personal inclinations I may not ignore it. Let us return into the tavern; I now require from you all factual information.'

For an hour the discussion continued, Etzwane politely persistent, Ifness formal, rational, and impervious as a block of glass. Under no circumstances would he attempt to procure for Etzwane a vehicle of the type he had in mind.

'In that case,' said Etzwane, 'I will proceed with less efficient transportation.'

The statement surprised Ifness. 'You seriously intend to venture into Caraz? Such a journey might occupy two or three years – assuming day-to-day survival.'

'I have taken all this into account,' said Etzwane. 'Naturally I will not trudge afoot through Caraz. I intend to fly.'

'By balloon? By glider?' Ifness raised his eyebrows. 'Across the wilds of Caraz?'

'Long ago the folk of Shant built a combination craft, the so-called "Farway". The fuselage and wing roots were gas-inflated; the wings were long and flexible. Such a craft is heavy enough to glide, but light enough to stay aloft on a breath.'

Ifness toyed with a silver trinket. 'And once you touch ground?'

'I am vulnerable, but not helpless. A man, single-handed, can kite himself up in an ordinary glider; still, he must wait for wind. The Farway rises against an easy breeze. The voyage will be a risk, I agree.'

'A risk? Suicide.'

Etzwane nodded somberly. 'I would prefer the use of a power vehicle such as Dasconetta might supply.'

Ifness gave the silver trinket a petulant jerk. 'Return here tomorrow. I will arrange for air transportation. You will be under my orders.'

For the folk of Shant the affairs of the next canton were of small concern; Caraz was as far as the Schiafarilla*

* Schiafarilla: a cluster of two thousand magnificent stars which illuminated the summer nights of Shant. The Earth worlds lay on the far side of the Schiafarilla.

and not nearly so visible. Etzwane, a musician, had traveled every region of Shant and was somewhat wider in his viewpoints; nevertheless Caraz was to him no more than a far region of windy wastes, mountains, and chasms of incomprehensible scale. The rivers of Caraz straddled vast plains, brimming too wide to be seen from bank to bank. Durdane, nine thousand years before, had been settled by fugitives, recalcitrants, and dissidents; the wildest and most irredeemable had fled to Caraz to lose themselves forever, wandering from one hazy distance into the next. Their descendants still roamed the solitudes.

At noon Etzwane returned to Fontenay's Inn, but found no sign of Ifness. An hour passed, and another. Etzwane went outside and paced up and down the avenue. His mood was placid, if somewhat heavy. Irritation towards Ifness, so he had concluded, was self-defeating. As well feel anger towards the three suns.

Ifness at last appeared, striding up Galias Avenue from the direction of the Sualle. His face was set in long, pensive lines; for a moment it seemed as if he would walk past Etzwane without acknowledgment, but at the last moment he stopped short. 'You wanted to meet Dasconetta,' said Ifness. 'So you shall. Wait here; I will be no more than a moment.'

He stepped into the tavern. Etzwane looked up into the sky as a bank of clouds passed before the suns; gloom pervaded the city. Etzwane frowned and shivered.

Ifness returned, wearing a black cloak which flapped dramatically as he walked. 'Come,' said Ifness, and turned up the avenue.

Etzwane, thinking to assert his dignity, made no move to follow. 'Where?'

Ifness swung about, eyes glittering. He spoke in an even voice. 'In a joint enterprise each party must learn what to expect from the other. From me you may count on information adequate to the needs of the moment; I will not burden you with over-elaboration. From you I will expect alertness, discretion, and responsiveness. We will now proceed, to Canton Wild Rose.'

Etzwane felt he had won at least a minor concession, and went silently with Ifness to the balloon-way station.

The balloon *Karmoune* tugged at the guys; immediately upon Ifness and Etzwane's stepping into the gondola, the ground crew loosed the judas-dolly; the balloon swung aloft. The winch-tender canted to the beam wind; the *Karmoune* fled south, dolly singing in the slot.

Through Jardeen Gap they flew, with the Ushkadel bulking to either side. Etzwane glimpsed the palace of the Sershans glittering through the forest of similax and cypress. The pleasant vales of Canton Wild Rose spread before them and presently they came to the town Jamilo. The *Karmoune* showed an orange semaphore; the ground crew shackled the running-dolly and walked the judas-dolly to the depot, bringing the *Karmoune* down to the landing ramp. Ifness and Etzwane alighted; Ifness signaled a diligence. He gave the driver a terse order; the two climbed aboard and the pacer* sprang off down the road.

For half an hour they drove up the Jardeen Valley, past the country places of the Garwiy Aesthetes,† then through an orchard of strawberry trees to an ancient manor house. Ifness spoke to Etzwane in a measured voice. 'You may be asked questions. I cannot suggest your responses, but be succinct and volunteer no information.'

* Pacer: a draft beast evolved from bullocks brought to Durdane by the first settlers. Horses similarly imported died of gland fever or were killed by ahulphs.

† The construction of the glass city Garwiy was controlled by the Aesthetic Society, which eventually became a caste of hereditary nobility, the Aesthetes.

'I have nothing to hide,' said Etzwane, somewhat curtly. 'If I am questioned, I will answer as my best judgment advises.'

Ifness made no reply.

The diligence halted in the shadow of an old-style observation tower. The two men alighted; Ifness led the way through a rank garden, across a courtyard paved with pale-green marble, into the front hall of the manor. He halted and signaled Etzwane to do likewise. No sound was to be heard; the house seemed deserted. The air smelled of dust, dry wood, old varnish. A shaft of lavender afternoon light slanted down through a high window to play on a faded portrait of a child in the quaint costume of olden times . . . At the end of the hall a man appeared. For a moment he stood watching, then came a step forward. Ignoring Etzwane, he spoke to Ifness in a suave, rhythmical language, to which Ifness made a brief reply. The two moved away and passed through a doorway; Etzwane unobtrusively followed, into a tall, twelve-sided room paneled in snuff-brown madera and illuminated by six high bull's-eyes of dusty purple glass. Etzwane examined the man with candid interest. Could he be Dasconetta, living like a ghost in this ancient house? Strange, if not incredible. He was a strongly built man of middle size, abrupt but tightly controlled of movement. A pelt of glossy black hair formed a prow halfway down his high and prominent forehead, then coved back from the temples, and again around the ears. His nose and chin were pallid; his mouth showed almost no lip whatever. After a single flash of his black eyes, he paid Etzwane no further attention.

Ifness and Dasconetta (if this were his identity) spoke in measured sentences, Ifness stating, Dasconetta acknowledging. Etzwane settled upon a camphorwood bench and watched the conversation. There was clearly no friendship between the two men. Ifness was not so much on the defensive as wary; Dasconetta listened attentively, as if matching each word against a previous statement or point of view. On one occasion Ifness half-turned towards Etzwane, as if to command corroboration or to draw forth some special fact; Dasconetta halted him with a wry word.

Ifness set forth a demand, which Dasconetta rejected. Ifness persisted and now Dasconetta performed a strange act: he reached behind him and by some unknown method brought into view a square four-foot panel composed of a thousand blinking white and gray shapes. Ifness made a set of remarks, to which Dasconetta gave a reply. Both examined the square panel, which blinked and flickered black, gray, and white. Dasconetta turned back to face Ifness with a quiet smile.

The conversation continued another five minutes. Dasconetta spoke the final sentence; Ifness turned away, walked from the room. Etzwane followed.

Ifness marched silently back to the diligence. Etzwane, controlling his exasperation, asked, 'What have you learned?'

'Nothing new. The policy group will not approve my plans.'

Etzwane looked back at the old manor, wondering why Dasconetta would choose to make his headquarters here. He asked, 'What then is to be done?'

'About what?'

'About a vehicle to take us to Caraz.'

Ifness said in an offhand voice, 'That is not my primary concern. Transportation can be contrived if and when needful.'

Etzwane struggled to maintain an even voice. 'What then was your "primary concern"?'

'I suggested an investigation by agencies other than the

Historical Institute. Dasconetta and his clique are unwilling to risk an adulteration of the environment. As you saw, Dasconetta was able to manipulate a consensus.'

'What of Dasconetta? Does he reside permanently here in Wild Rose?'

Ifness allowed a small twitch of a smile to his lips. 'Dasconetta is far away, beyond the Schiafarilla. You saw his simula; he spoke to mine. The business is accomplished by a scientific method.'

Etzwane looked back towards the old house. 'And who is there?'

'No one. It is joined to a similar structure on the world Glantzen Five.'

They climbed into the diligence, which set off towards Jamilo.

Etzwane said, 'Your conduct is incomprehensible. Why did you assert that you could not take us to Caraz?'

'I made no such assertion,' said Ifness. 'You drew a faulty inference, for which I cannot accept responsibility. In any event the situation is more complicated than you suppose, and you must be prepared for subtlety.'

'Subtlety or deception?' demanded Etzwane. 'The effect is much the same.'

Ifness held up his hand. 'I will explain the situation, if only to reduce the flow of your reproaches . . . I conferred with Dasconetta neither to persuade him nor to requisition transportation, but, rather, to provoke his adoption of an incorrect policy. He has now made this error, and furthermore obtained a consensus through the use of incomplete and subjective information. The way is open for a demonstration to cut the ground out from under his feet. When I make an investigation I will be acting outside Standard Procedures, which will embarrass Dasconetta and catch him in a dilemma. He must commit himself even more completely to an obviously incorrect position or perform a humiliating reversal.'

Etzwane gave a skeptical grunt. 'Has not Dasconetta taken all this into consideration?'

'I think not. He would hardly have called for a consensus and argued from so rigid a position. He is sure of his case, which is based on Institute Regulation; he imagines me fretting and constrained. The opposite is true; he has opened the door upon a set of rewarding prospects.

Etzwane was unable to share Ifness' enthusiasm. 'Only if the investigation yields significant results.'

Ifness shrugged. 'If the rumors are incorrect, I am no worse off than before, except for the stigma of the consensus, which Dasconetta planned in any event.'

'I see . . . Why did you take me to this encounter?'

'I hoped that Dasconetta might question you, in order to embarrass me further. He cautiously decided against this procedure.'

'Hmmf.' Etzwane was not flattered by the role which Ifness had laid out for him. 'So now what do you plan?'

'I intend to study the events which purportedly have occurred in Caraz. The affair puzzles me: why should the asutra test the Roguskhoi again? They are a faulty concept; why deploy them a second time? Who are the men who used energy weapons in the rumored battle? Certainly not Palasedrans, certainly not men of Shant. There is mystery here; I confess that I am tantalised. So now, tell me: exactly where did this rumored engagement occur? It is agreed that we will join forces for this particular investigation.'

'Near the settlement Shillinsk, on the Keba River.'

'I will check my references tonight. Tomorrow we will depart. There is no room for delay.'

Etzwane became silent. The reality of the situation now faced him; he felt a mood of awe and presentiment. In a thoughtful voice he said, 'I will be ready.'

Late in the evening Etzwane once more called upon Aun Sharah, who showed no surprise to learn of Etzwane's plans. 'I can supply another trifle – no, two trifles – of information. The first is negative, in that we have spoken to mariners from other shores of Caraz. None mention Roguskhoi. The second item is a rather vague report of spaceships, which might or might not have been sighted in the Orgai region, west of the Kuzi Kaza. The report goes no further than this. I wish you good luck and will anxiously await your return. I understand your motives but I doubt if they would persuade me to venture into central Caraz.'

Etzwane gave a hollow chuckle. 'I have nothing better to do at the moment.'

Chapter 3

Etzwane arrived early at Fontenay's Inn. He wore a suit of gray hard-cloth, a jacket of water-repellent bast against the mists and rains of Caraz, ankle boots of chumpa* leather. In his pouch he carried the energy gun Ifness had given him long ago.

Ifness was nowhere upon the premises. Once again Etzwane walked fretfully up and down the avenue. An hour passed; then a diligence drew up beside him. The driver signaled. 'You are Gastel Etzwane? Please come with me.'

Etzwane scrutinised the man with suspicion. 'Where?'

'To a place north of the city; such are my instructions.'

'Who instructed you?'

'A certain Ifness.'

Etzwane entered the diligence. They drove north beside the Jardeen estuary, which presently spread wide to become the Sualle. The city fell behind; they followed a waterfront road through a dreary wasteland of rubble, nettles, sheds and warehouses, and a few dilapidated cabins. At an ancient house built of slag bricks the diligence halted. The driver made a sign; Etzwane alighted. The diligence drove back the way it had come.

* Chumpa: a large, indigenous animal similar to the quasi-biped ahulphs but less intelligent and characterised by a ferocious disposition.

Etzwane knocked on the door of the house, evoking no response. He went around to the back, where at the foot of a rocky slope a boathouse extended over the water. Etzwane followed a path down the slope and looked into the boathouse, to find Ifness loading parcels into a sail boat.

Etzwane stood wondering if Ifness had lost his faculties. To sail such a boat across the Green Ocean, around the north coast of Caraz to Erbol, thence up the Keba River to Burnoun was, to say the least, impractical, if for no other reason than the length of the journey.

Ifness seemed to read his mind. In a dry voice he said, 'By the very nature of our research, we cannot fly grandly about Caraz in an air-yacht. Are you ready to depart? If so, step into the boat.'

'I am ready.' Etzwane took himself aboard the boat. Ifness cast off the mooring lines and pushed the boat out upon the face of the Sualle. 'Be so good as to raise the sail.'

Etzwane heaved upon the halyard; the sail billowed; the boat moved out upon the water. Etzwane seated himself gingerly upon a thwart and considered the receding shore. He glanced into the cabin at the parcels Ifness had brought aboard and wondered what they contained. Food and drink? Enough for three days, at the most a week. Etzwane shrugged and looked out over the Sualle. Suns' light glinted from ten million cat's-paws in thirty million pink, blue, and white sparks. Astern rose the wonderful glass shapes of Garwiy, colors muted by distance. He might never see the glass towers of Garwiy again.

For an hour the boat sailed out upon the Sualle until the shores were indistinct and no other boats could be seen. Ifness said curtly, 'You may lower the sail and then unship the mast.'

Etzwane obeyed. Ifness meanwhile brought forth sections of transparent stuff, which he fitted into a windscreen around the cockpit. Etzwane watched silently. Ifness made a last survey around the horizon, then raised the cover from a cuddy at the stern. Etzwane noticed a black panel, a set of white, red, and blue knobs. Ifness made an adjustment. The boat lifted into the air, dripping water, then slanted into the sky. Ifness touched the knobs; the boat curved west, to fly high over the mud flats of Fenesq. Ifness said in a casual voice, 'A boat is the least conspicuous vehicle in which to travel; it arouses attention nowhere, not even in Caraz.'

'An ingenious artifice,' said Etzwane.

Ifness nodded indifferently. 'I lack accurate charts and we must navigate by rule of thumb. Shant maps are only guesses. We will follow the Caraz coast to the mouth of the Keba River, something over two thousand miles, so I should reckon. We can then follow the Keba south without risk of losing our way.'

Etzwane recalled the great map in the Jurdisdictionary. In the general area of Shillinsk he had noticed several rivers; the Panjorek, the Blue Zura, the Black Zura, the Usak, the Bobol. To attempt an overland short cut was to risk coming down upon the wrong river. He turned his attention down upon the flatlands of Canton Fenesq, tracing the canals and waterways which radiated from the four Fen towns. The cantonal border appeared in the distance: a line of black alyptus trees; beyond the bogs and moors of Canton Gitanesq extended into purple murk.

Ifness, crouching in the cabin, brewed a pot of tea. Sitting up under the forward screen, with wind hissing overhead, the two drank tea and ate nut cakes from one of the parcels Ifness had brought aboard. Etzwane thought that Ifness seemed relaxed and almost genial. To attempt a conversation was to risk rebuff, but now Ifness himself vouchsafed a remark. 'Well, we are off in good style and without interference from any source.'

'Did you expect any?'

'Not seriously. I doubt if the asutra maintain agents in Shant; the area can be of little real interest to them. Dasconetta might have placed an information with the Institute monitors, but I believe we were too quick for them.'

'Your relationship with Dasconetta seems awkward indeed.'

Ifness gave a nod of acquiescence. 'In an organisation such as the Institute, a Fellow achieves status by demonstrating judgment superior to that of his colleagues, particularly those who are reckoned astute. I have outmaneuvered Dasconetta so decisively that I begin to be worried: what is he up to? How can he thwart me without endorsing my viewpoint? It is a dangerous and complicated business.'

Etzwane frowned sidewise at Ifness, whose motivations and attitudes, as usual, he found incomprehensible. 'Dasconetta concerns me less than our work in Caraz, which perhaps is not so complicated but equally dangerous. Dasconetta, after all, is neither a ritual murderer nor a cannibal.'

'Such acts have not been proved against him, certainly,' said Ifness with a faint smile. 'Well well, perhaps you are right. I must turn my attention to Caraz. According to Kreposkin* the region of the middle Keba is relatively placid, especially north of the Urt Unna foothills. Shillinsk would seem to lie within this area. He mentions river pirates and a local tribe, the Sorukh. On the river islands live the degenerate Gorioni, whom even the slavers ignore.'

Below rose the Hurra Hills, and where the Cliffs of Day hurled back the swells of the Green Ocean, Shant came to an end. For an hour they flew over blank, empty water, then at the horizon appeared a vague dark mark: Caraz. Etzwane stirred himself. Ifness sat with his back to the

* Kreposkin, *The Kingdoms of Old Caraz.*

wind, cogitating over his notebook. Etzwane asked, 'How do you propose to conduct the investigation?'

Ifness closed his notebook, looked over the side and around the sky before replying. 'I have no specific plans. We are setting out to solve a mystery. First we must gather facts, then draw our conclusions. At the moment we know very little. The Roguskhoi seem to have been artificially developed as an antihuman weapon. The asutra who control them are a parasitical race, or, more sympathetically, might be said to live in symbiosis with their hosts. The Roguskhoi failed in Shant. Why do we find them in Caraz? To conquer territory? To guard a colony? Develop a resource? At the moment we can only wonder.

Caraz dominated the western horizon. Ifness swung the boat a point or two north and slanted gradually against the shoreline. Late in the afternoon mud flats appeared below, marked by tremulous wisps of surf. Ifness adjusted course and all night the boat drifted at half-speed along the coast, following trails of phosphorescent foam. Predawn murk discovered the hulk of Cape Comranus ahead, and Ifness pronounced Kreposkin's maps worthless. 'Essentially he informs us only that a Cape Comranus exists, that it is to be found somewhere along the Caraz shore. We must use these maps with skepticism.'

All morning the boat followed the coast, which after Cape Comranus had veered eastward, past a succession of crouching headlands separated by mud flats. At noon they flew over a peninsula of barren stone extending fifty miles north, unidentified on Kreposkin's maps; then the sea returned. Ifness allowed the boat to descend until they drifted only a thousand feet above the beach.

Halfway through the afternoon they crossed the mouth of a vast river: the Gever, draining the Geverman Basin, into which the whole of Shant might have been fitted. A village of a hundred stone cabins occupied the lee of a hill; a dozen boats swung at anchor. This was the first habitation they had seen on Caraz.

Persuaded by Kreposkin's map, Ifness turned the boat westward and inland, across a densely forested wilderness extending north past the reach of vision: the Mirv Peninsula. A hundred miles fell astern. From an almost invisible clearing a wisp of smoke lazed up into the air. Etzwane glimpsed three timber cabins, and for ten minutes he looked astern, wondering what sort of men and women lived lost in this northern forest of Caraz . . . Another hundred miles passed, and they came to the far shore of the Mirv Peninsula, in this case to validate Kreposkin's map. Once again they flew over water. Ahead the estuary of the Hietze River opened into the land: a cleft twenty miles wide studded with steep-sided islands, each a miniature fairyland of delightful trees and mossy meadows. One of the islands supported a gray stone castle; beside another a cargo vessel lay moored.

During the late afternoon, clouds rolled down from the north; plum-colored gloom fell across the landscape. Ifness slowed the boat and upon consideration descended to a sheltered crescent of beach. As lightning began to lash the sky, Etzwane and Ifness rigged a tarpaulin over the cockpit, then, with rain drumming on the fabric, they drank tea and ate a meal of bread and meat. Etzwane asked, 'Suppose the asutra attacked Durdane with spaceships and powerful weapons: what would the people of the Earth worlds do? Would they send warships to protect us?'

Ifness leaned back against the thwart. 'These are unpredictable matters. The Coordinating Board is a conservative group; the worlds are absorbed in their own affairs. The Pan-Humanic League is no longer influential, if ever it was. Durdane is far away and forgotten; the

Shciafarilla intervenes. The Coordination might make a representation, depending upon a report from the Historical Institute, which enjoys prestige. Dasconetta, for purposes to which I have alluded, seeks to minimise the situation. He will not acknowledge that the asutra are the first technologically competent nonhuman creatures we have encountered, a highly important occasion.'

'Curious! The facts speak for themselves.'

'True. But there is more to it, as you might guess. Dasconetta and his clique advocate caution and further research; in due course they propose to issue the announcement under their own aegis; I will never be mentioned. This scheme must be thwarted.'

Etzwane, engaged in rueful reflections regarding the quality of Ifness' concern, went to look out into the night. The rain had dwindled to a few dark drops; the lightning flickered far to the east, back over the Mirv. Etzwane listened, but could hear no sound whatever. Ifness also stepped out to look at the night.

'We might proceed, but I am uncertain in regard to the Keba and the intervening rivers. Kreposkin is exasperating in that he can neither be totally scorned nor totally trusted. Best that we wait for the light.' He stood peering through the dark. 'According to Kreposkin, yonder along the beach is the site of Suserane, a town built by the Shelm Fyrids some six thousand years ago . . . Caraz, then as now, was savage and vast. No matter how many enemies fell in battle, more always came. One or another warrior tribe laid Suserane waste; now there is nothing left: only the influences Kreposkin calls *esmeric.*'

'I do not know that word.'

'It derives from a dialect of old Caraz and means the association or atmosphere clinging to a place: the unseen ghosts, the dissipated sounds, the suffused glory, music, tragedy, exultation, grief, and terror, which according to Kreposkin never dissipates.'

Etzwane looked through the dark towards the site of the old city; if *esmeric* were present, it worked but weakly through the dark. Etzwane returned to the boat and tried to sleep on the narrow starboard berth.

The morning sky was clear. The blue sun, Etta, swung up near the horizon, producing a false blue dawn, then pink Sasetta slanted sidewise into the sky, then white Zael, and again blue Etta. After a breakfast of tea and dried fruit, and a cursory glance at the site of old Suserane, Ifness took the boat into the air. Ahead, dull as lead in the light from the east, a great river mouth gaped into the mass of Caraz. Ifness named the river the Usak. At noon they passed the Bobol, and at midafternoon reached the mouth of the Keba, which Ifness identified by the chalk cliffs along the western shore and the trading post Erbol, five miles inland.

Ifness swung south over the watercourse, here forty miles wide with three sun trails across the brimming surface. The river seemed to curve somewhat to the right, then at the horizon's verge it swept majestically back to the left. Three barges, miniscule from the height, floated on the face of the river, two inching upstream to the force of billowing square sails, another drifting downstream with the current.

'The charts are of small benefit henceforth,' said Ifness. 'Kreposkin mentions no settlements along the middle Keba, although he refers to the Sorukh race, a warlike folk who never turn their backs in battle.'

Etzwane studied Kreposkin's rude maps. 'Two thousand miles south along the river, into the Burnoun district: that would take us about here, to the Plain of Blue Flowers.'

Ifness was not interested in Etzwane's opinions. 'The maps are only approximations,' he said crisply. 'We will fly a certain distance, then undertake a local investigation.' He closed the book and turning away became absorbed in his own thoughts.

Etzwane smiled a trifle grimly. He had become accustomed to Ifness' mannerisms and no longer allowed himself to become wrathful. He went forward and looked out over the tremendous purple forests, the pale-blue distances, the bogs and swamps of mottled green, and, dominating the landscape, the flood of the river Keba. Here was where he had come, to wild Caraz, because he feared staleness and insipidity. What of Ifness? What had urged the fastidious Ifness to such vicissitudes? Etzwane started to ask the question, then he held his tongue; Ifness would give a mordant answer, with Etzwane none the better informed.

Etzwane turned and looked south, into Caraz, where so many mysteries awaited illumination.

The boat flew all night, holding its course by the reflection of the blazing Schiafarilla upon the river. At noon Ifness lowered the boat towards the river, which here ran irregularly about ten miles wide, swelling, narrowing, and encompassing a myriad of wooded islands.

'Be on the lookout for habitation, or even better, a riverboat,' Ifness told Etzwane. 'We now require local information.'

'How will you understand? The folk of Caraz speak an outlandish yammer.'

'Nonetheless, we will manage, or so I believe,' said Ifness in his most didactic drawl. 'The Burnoun and the Keba Basin are linguistically uniform. The folk use a dialect derived from the language of Shant.'

Etzwane looked sidewise in disbelief. 'How can this be? Shant is far distant.'

'The circumstance derives from the Third Palasedran War. Cantons Maseach, Gorgach, and Parthe collaborated with the Eagle Dukes, and many folk, dreading Pandamon vengeance, fled Shant. They made their way up the Keba and imposed their language on the Sorukhs, who ultimately enslaved them. The history of Caraz is far from cheerful.' Ifness leaned over the gunwales and pointed to a straggle of huts on the riverbank, hardly to be seen behind a covert of tall reeds. 'A village, where we can gain information, even if only negative.' He reflected. 'We will employ a harmless hoax to facilitate the matter. These people are indomitably superstitious and will enjoy a demonstration of their beliefs.' He adjusted a dial; the boat slowed and hung motionless in mid-air. 'Let us now ship the mast and raise the sail, then make a change or two in our costume.'

Down from the sky floated the boat, sail billowing, with Etzwane at the tiller ostensibly steering. Both he and Ifness wore white turbans and carried themselves in a portentous manner. The boat settled upon the flat before the huts, still puddled from the rainstorm of two days before. A half-dozen men stood stock-still; as many slatternly women peered from the doorways; naked children crawling in the mud froze in place or backed whimpering away to shelter. Stepping from the boat, Ifness sprinkled a handful of blue and green glass gems upon the ground. He pointed to a portly elder who stood dumbfounded at hand. 'Approach, if you please,' spoke Ifness in a coarse dialect barely intelligible to Etzwane. 'We are benevolent wizards and intend you no harm; we want information in regard to our enemies.'

The old man's chin trembled, agitating his dirty whiskers; he clutched his ragged homespun tunic about his belly and essayed a few steps forward. 'What information do you require? We are only clamdiggers, no more; we know nothing beyond the flow of the river.'

'Just so,' intoned Ifness. 'Still, you are witness to comings and goings, and I notice a shed yonder for the storage of trade goods.'

'Yes, we have modest dealings in clam cake, clam wine, and crushed clamshell of good quality. But for knowledge of loot or precious things you must ask elsewhere. Even the slavers pass us by.'

'We seek news of a tribe of invading warriors: large, red-skinned demons who slaughter men and copulate with the women to notorious degree. These are the Roguskhoi. Have you had news regarding these folk?'

'They have not troubled us, the Sacred Eel be thanked. The traders tell us of fighting and an epic battle, but in all my life I have heard nothing else, and no one has used the name "Roguskhoi".'

'Where then was the fighting?'

The clamdigger pointed south. 'The Sorukh regions are still far: it is ten days' sail to the Plain of Blue Flowers, though your magic boat will speed you there in half the time . . . Are you permitted to teach the lore which propels your craft? It would be a great convenience for me.'

'Such a question best had not be asked,' said Ifness. 'We now proceed to the Plain of Blue Flowers.'

'May the Eel expedite your passage.'

Ifness stepped back into the boat, gave Etzwane a formal signal. Etzwane worked the rudder and adjusted the sheets, while Ifness touched his controls. The boat rose, the sails caught the wind; the boat sailed off across the river. The men ran down to the water's edge to stare after them, followed by the children and women from the huts. Ifness chuckled. 'We have made memorable at least one day of their lives, and fractured a dozen rules of the Institute.'

'Ten days' journey,' mused Etzwane. 'The barges move two or three miles an hour: fifty miles a day, more or less. Ten days' journey would be five hundred miles.'

'By just such a degree are Kreposkin's charts inaccurate.' Standing up in the cockpit Ifness raised his arm in a final flourish of benign farewell to the gaping folk of the village. A grove of waterwood trees hid them from sight. Ifness spoke over his shoulder to Etzwane: 'Lower the sail; unship the mast.'

Etzwane silently obeyed the command, reflecting that Ifness seemed to enjoy the role of wandering magician. The boat moved south up the river. Silver-trunked almacks lined the bank, their silver-purple fronds glinting green to the motion of the breeze. To right and left flatlands disappeared into the dove-gray haze of distance, and always the great Keba reached out ahead.

Afternoon waned; and the banks remained desolate of life, to Ifness' muttered disgust. The sun sank; twilight fell across the landscape. Ifness stood precariously on the foredeck, peering down into the dark. At last an array of flickering red sparks appeared on the riverbank. Ifness swung the boat around and down; the sparks became a dozen leaping campfires, arrayed in a rough circle, twenty or thirty yards in diameter.

'Ship the mast,' said Ifness. 'Hoist the sail.'

Etzwane thoughtfully appraised the fires and the folk who worked within the circle of light. Beyond he glimpsed large carts with crooked eight-foot wheels and leather hoods; they had come upon a band of nomads, of a temperament presumably more edgy and truculent than the placid clamdiggers. Etzwane looked dubiously towards Ifness, who stood like a statue. Very well, thought Etzwane, he would indulge Ifness in his mad jokes, even at the risk of flowing blood. He set up the mast, lifted the great square sail, then adjusting his turban, went back to the tiller.

The boat settled into the circle of firelight. Ifness called down, 'Beware below; move aside.'

The tribesmen looked up; jumping and cursing they sprang back. An old man tripped and spilled a tub of water upon a group of women, who screamed in fury.

The boat landed; Ifness with a stern mien held up his hand. 'Quiet! We are only two wizards of the night. Have you never seen magic before? Where is the chief of the clan?'

No one spoke. The men, in loose white shirts, baggy black breeches and black boots, stood back, uncertain whether to flee or attack. The women, in loose patterned gowns, wailed and showed the whites of their eyes.

'Who is the chief?' bawled Ifness. 'Can he not hear? Can he not walk forward?'

A hulking, black-browed man with black mustaches came slowly forward. 'I am Rastipol, chief of the Ripchiks. What do you want of me?'

'Why are you here and not fighting the Roguskhoi?'

' "Roguskhoi"?' Rastipol blinked. 'Who are they? We fight no one at this moment.'

'The Roguskhoi are red demon-warriors. They are only half human, though they show enthusiasm for human women.'

'I have heard of them. They fight the Sorukh; it is none of our affair. We are not Sorukh; we are out of the Melch race.'

'And if they destroy the Sorukh, what next?'

Rastipol scratched his chin. 'I have not considered the matter.'

'Exactly where has the fighting occurred?'

'Somewhere to the south, out on the Plain of Blue Flowers, or so I suppose.'

'How far is this?'

'Four days to the south is Shillinsk Town, at the edge of the Plain. Can you not learn this by magic?'

Ifness raised a finger towards Etzwane. 'Transform Rastipol into a sick ahulph.'

'No, no,' cried Rastipol. 'You have misjudged me. I meant no harm.'

Ifness gave a distant nod. 'Guard your tongue; you allow it a dangerous freedom.' He signaled Etzwane. 'Sail on.'

Etzwane worked the tiller and waved his hand towards the sail, while Ifness moved his dials. The boat lifted into the night sky, showing its keel to the firelight. The Ripchiks watched silently from below.

During the night the boat drifted slowly south. Etzwane slept on one of the narrow berths; he was not aware whether or not Ifness did the same. In the morning, cold and cramped, he went out into the cockpit to find Ifness looking out over the gunwale. A mist concealed the land below, the boat floated alone between gray mist and lavender sky.

For an hour the two sat in dour silence, drinking tea. At last the three suns rolled high and the mist began to dissipate, swirling and drifting, revealing irregular districts of land and river. Below them, the Keba made a mighty swing to the west, where it was joined from the east by a tributary, the Shill. On the west bank three docks thrust out into the Keba, marking a settlement of fifty or sixty huts and a half-dozen larger structures. Ifness exclaimed in satisfaction. 'Shillinsk at last! It exists in spite of Kreposkin!' He lowered the boat to the face of the water. Etzwane stepped the mast and hoisted the sail;

the boat proceeded across the water to the docks. Ifness brought the boat up the water-steps; Etzwane jumped ashore with a line; Ifness followed more deliberately. Etzwane payed out the line; the boat drifted downstream and took a place among a dozen fishing smacks, not notably different from itself. Ifness and Etzwane turned towards Shillinsk Town.

Chapter 4

The cabins and sheds of Shillinsk were built from gray stone quarried from a near-by ledge and rough-laid between balks of driftwood. Directly behind the docks stood the Shillinsk Inn, a relatively imposing structure of three stories. Lavender suns' light glared on gray stone and black timber; the shadows, by some ocular accommodation, appeared green, the color of old water in a barrel.

Shillinsk Town seemed quiet, only half alive. No sound could be heard except the lap of waves along the shore. Two women walked slowly along the riverside trail; they wore baggy black breeches, blouses of dark purple, headkerchiefs of rich rust-orange. Three barges lay alongside the docks, one empty and two partially laden. Several barge-tenders were bound for the tavern; Ifness and Etzwane followed a few paces to the rear.

The barge-tenders pushed through the driftwood doors, with Ifness and Etzwane behind them, into a common room considerably more comfortable than the rude exterior suggested. A fire of sea-coal blazed in a huge fireplace; the walls had been plastered, whitewashed, and decorated with festoons and rosettes of carved wood. A group of barge-tenders sat before the fire eating a stew of fish and reed root. To the side, half in the shadows, two men of the district sat hunched over their wooden mugs. Firelight molded their slab-sided faces; they spoke little and peered distrustfully sidewise, watching the barge-tenders. One displayed a black mustache bushy as a dust brush, the other wore both a chin beard and a two-inch copper nose ring. With fascination Etzwane saw him knock up the ring with the rim of his mug and drink. They wore the Sorukh costume: black breeches, loose shirts embroidered with fetish signs, and from their waists hung scimitars of the white metal *ghisim*, an alloy of silver, platinum, tin, and copper, forged and hardened by a secret process.

Ifness and Etzwane settled at a table near the fire. The innkeeper, a man bald and flat-faced, with a deformed leg and a hard stare, hobbled over to learn their wants. Ifness spoke for lodging and the best meal available. The innkeeper announced that he could serve clam soup, herbs, and sweet beetles; grilled meat with water-greens, bread, blue-flower marmalade, and vervain tea: a meal which Ifness had not expected and which he pronounced satisfactory.

'I must discuss my recompense,' said the innkeeper. 'What do you have to trade?'

Ifness brought forth one of his glass jewels. 'This.'

The innkeeper drew back and showed the palm of his hand in disdain. 'What do you take me for? This is no more than coarse glass, a bauble for children.'

'Indeed then,' said Ifness. 'What is its color?'

'It is the color of old grass, verging towards river water.'

'Look.' Ifness closed the gem in his hand, then opened it. 'What color now?'

'A clear crimson!'

'And now?' Ifness exposed the gem to the warmth of the fire and it glinted green as an emerald. 'Now – take it into the dark and tell me what you see.'

The innkeeper went off to a closet, and presently returned. 'It shines blue and sends off rays of several colors.'

'The object is a starstone,' said Ifness. 'Such are occasionally taken from the center of meteorites. It is in fact too valuable to exchange for mere food and lodging, but we have nothing else.'

'It will suffice, or so I suppose,' stated the landlord in a pompous voice. 'How long does your barge remain at Shillinsk?'

'Several days, until we conclude our business. We deal in exotic goods, and at this moment we required the neck bones of dead Roguskhoi, which have a medicinal efficacy.'

' "Roguskhoi"? What are they?'

'You call them differently. I refer to the red, half-human warriors which have pillaged the Plain of Blue Flowers.'

'Ah! We call them the "Red Devils". They are of value after all?'

'I make no such assertions; I merely traffic in bones. Who would be the local dealer in such merchandise?'

The innkeeper uttered a coarse bark of laughter, which he quickly stifled, and turned a look towards the two Sorukh, who had been attending the conversation.

'In these parts,' said the inkeeper, 'bones are so common as to be worthless, and a man's life is at little greater price. Observe this leg, which my mother maimed to protect me from the slave-takers. They were then the Esche from the Murd Mountains across the Shill. Now the Esche are gone and Hulkas have come, and all is as before, or worse. Never turn your back to a Hulka, or you'll find a chain around your neck. Four from Shillinsk have been taken during this last year. Hulka or Red Devil – which is worse? Take your choice.'

The mustached Sorukh suddenly joined the talk. 'The Red Devils are extinct, except for their bones, which as you know belong to us.'

'Precisely the case,' declared the second Sorukh, the ring swinging against his lip as he spoke. 'We know the therapeutic effect of Red Devil bones, and we intend to realise a fair profit.'

'All very well,' said Ifness, 'but why do you assert their extinction?'

'The matter is common knowledge across the Plain.'

'And who accomplished this act?'

The Sorukh tugged at his beard. 'The Hulkas perhaps, or a band from over the Kuzi Kaza. It seems that magic was worked on both sides.'

'The Hulkas lack magic,' remarked the innkeeper. 'They are ordinary slavers. The tribes beyond the Kuzi Kaza are ferocious, but I have never heard magic ascribed to them.'

The ring-nosed Sorukh made a sudden harsh gesture. 'This is not germane.' He turned to Ifness. 'Do you intend to buy our bones, or shall we take them elsewhere?'

'I naturally want to inspect them,' said Ifness. 'Let us go look, then we can talk more to the point.'

The Sorukhs sat back in shock. 'Here is absurdity taken to the point of offense. Do you think we carry merchandise on our backs like Tchark women? We are proud folk and resent an affront!'

'I intended no offense,' said Ifness. 'I merely expressed a desire to see the merchandise. Where is it stored?'

'Let us make a short matter of the situation,' said the Sorukh with the mustache. 'The bones remain at the battlefield, or so I suppose. We will sell our interest for a modest trade, and then you can do what you wish with the bones.'

Ifness thought a moment. 'This procedure is scarcely to my advantage. What if the bones are of poor quality? Or impossible to transport? Either bring the bones here or conduct us to the bones, so that I may judge their value.'

The Sorukhs became glum. Turning aside they muttered together. Ifness and Etzwane set upon the food served by the innkeeper. Etzwane, glancing towards the Sorukhs, said, 'They are only planning how best to murder us and take our wealth.'

Ifness nodded. 'They are also puzzled why we are not more concerned; they fear an unexpected trick. Still, they will never reject the bait.'

The Sorukhs reached a decision and watched through heavy-lidded eyes until Etzwane and Ifness had finished their meal, whereupon the Sorukhs moved to the adjoining table, bringing with them an organic waft. Ifness shifted position and regarded the two with his head thrown back. The Sorukh with the mustache essayed a friendly smile. 'Matters can be arranged to our mutual benefit. You are prepared to inspect the bones and pay for them on the spot?'

'Definitely not,' said Ifness. 'I will examine the bones and inform you if they are worth the transport here to Shillinsk.'

The Sorukh's smile lingered a second or two, then vanished. Ifness went on. 'Can you provide transportation? A comfortable cart drawn by pacers?'

The Sorukh with the ring in his nose gave a snort of disdain. 'That is not possible,' said the Sorukh with the mustache. 'The Kuzi Kaza would break up the cart.'

'Very well then; we will require riding pacers.'

The Sorukhs drew back. They muttered together, the ring-nosed man surly and unwilling, the man with the mustache first urgent, then persuasive, then compelling – and finally he had his way. They returned to Ifness and Etzwane. 'When will you be ready to depart?' asked the mustached man.

'Tomorrow morning, as early as feasible.'

'At sunrise we will be ready. But a further important

matter: you must pay a rent for the pacers.'

'Ridiculous on the face of it!' scoffed Ifness. 'I am not even sure that the bones exist! And you expect me to pay out rent on what might be a wild-goose chase? By no means; I was not born yesterday.'

The ring-nosed Sorukh started to make an angry argument, but the mustached man held up his hand. 'You will see the bones, and the pacer rent will be absorbed in the ultimate transaction.'

'That is more to the point,' said Ifness. 'Upon our return to Shillinsk we will arrange an inclusive price.'

'At sunrise we depart; be ready.' The two Sorukhs left the inn; Ifness sipped hot infusion from a wooden bowl.

Etzwane demanded: 'You plan to ride the plain on a pacer? Why not fly the boat?'

Ifness raised his eyebrows. 'Is the matter not self-evident? A boat in the middle of a dry plain is a conspicuous object. We would have no freedom of action; we could never leave the boat.'

'If we leave the boat at Shillinsk, we will never see it again,' grumbled Etzwane. 'These people are thieves, one and all.'

'I will make certain arrangements.' Ifness considered a moment, then crossed the room and spoke with the innkeeper. He returned and resumed his seat at the table. 'The innkeeper declares that we might leave ten treasure chests aboard our boat without fear of molestation. He accepts full responsibility, and the risk is thereby reduced.' Ifness mused a moment or two upon the flames of the fire. 'Nevertheless, I will arrange a warning device to discourage those pilferers who might escape his vigilance.'

Etzwane, who had no taste for an arduous ride across the Plain of Blue Flowers in company with the Sorukhs, said sourly, 'Instead of a flying boat, you should have contrived a flying cart, or a pair of flying pacers.'

'Your concepts have merit,' said Ifness benignly.

For the repose of its patrons the inn provided boxes filled with straw in a row of small chambers on the second floor. Etzwane's cubicle commanded a view of the harbor. The straw, however, was not fresh; during the night it rustled with obscure activity, and the previous occupant had urinated in a corner of the room. At midnight Etzwane, aroused by a sound, went to look out the window. He observed furtive motion along the dock, near the area where the boat was moored. The starlight was too dim for precise vision, but Etzwane noticed a hobbling irregularity in the gait of the skulker. The man stepped into a dinghy and rowed quietly out to the boat. He shipped his oars, made fast the dinghy, and clambered aboard the boat, to be instantly surrounded by tongues of blue flame, while sparks jumped from his hair to the rigging. The man danced across the deck and more by accident than design plunged overboard. A few moments later he feebly hauled himself into his dinghy and rowed back to the dock.

At sunrise Etzwane arose from his straw and went to the first-floor washroom, where he found Ifness. Etzwane reported the events of the night, regarding which Ifness showed no great surprise. 'I will see to the matter.'

For breakfast the innkeeper served only tea and bread. His limp was more pronounced than ever and he glowered spitefully towards Ifness as he banged the food down upon the table.

Ifness said sternly, 'This is spartan fare; are you so exhausted from your foray that you cannot provide a suitable breakfast?'

The innkeeper attempted a blustering retort, but Ifness cut him short. 'Do you know why you are here now, instead of dancing to the music of blue sparks? Because I require a satisfactory breakfast. Need I say more?'

'I have heard enough,' muttered the innkeeper. He hobbled back into the kitchen, and presently brought forth a cauldron of stewed fish, a tray of oatcake and eel-jelly. 'Will this appease your appetite? If not, I can furnish some good boiled ermink and a sack of cheese.'

'We have enough,' said Ifness. 'Remember, if on my return I find so much as a splinter of the boat disarranged, you shall dance again to the blue music.'

'You misinterpret my zeal,' declared the innkeeper. 'I rowed out to the boat because I thought I heard a suspicious noise.'

'The matter is at an end,' said Ifness indifferently, 'so long as now we understand each other.'

The two Sorukhs looked into the inn. 'Are you ready to depart? The pacers are waiting.'

Etzwane and Ifness went out into the cool morning. Four pacers pulled nervously at their curbs, hooking and slashing with back-curved horns. Etzwane considered them of good stock, long-limbed and deep-chested. They were equipped with nomad steppe-saddles of chumpa leather, with pouches for food and a rack on which a tent, blanket, and night boots might be lashed. The Sorukhs refused to provide these articles for Ifness and Etzwane. Threats and persuasion had no effect, and Ifness was forced to part with another of his multicolored jewels before the requisite food and equipment were supplied.

Before departure Ifness required the identities of the two Sorukhs. Both were of the Bellbird fetish in the Varsk clan; the mustached man was Gulshe; he of the ringed nose was Srenka. Ifness wrote the names in blue ink upon a strip of parchment. He added a set of marks in crimson and yellow, while the Sorukhs looked on uneasily. 'Why do you do this?' challenged Srenka.

'I take ordinary precautions,' said Ifness. 'I have left

my jewels in a secret place and now carry no valuables; search me if you care to do so. I have worked a curse upon your names, which I will lift in good time. Your plans to murder and rob us are unwise and had best be dismissed.'

Gulshe and Srenka scowled at what was obviously an unpleasant turn of events. 'Shall we be on our way?' suggested Ifness.

The four mounted and set off across the Plain of Blue Flowers.

The Keba, with its fringe of almacks, receded and at last was lost to sight. To all sides the plain rolled in great sweeps and swells out into the sunny lavender haze. Purple moss padded the soil; shrubs held aloft flowers which colored the plain a soft sea-blue in all directions. To the south appeared an almost imperceptible shadow of mountains.

All day the four men rode, and at nightfall made camp in a shallow swale beside a trickle of dank water. They sat around the fire in an atmosphere of guarded cordiality. It developed that Gulshe himself had skirmished with a band of the Roguskhoi only two months previously. 'They came down out of the Orgai Mountains, not far from Shagfe, where the Hulka maintain a slave depot. The Red Devils had raided the slave depot twice before, killing men and carrying off the women, and Hozman Sore-throat, the agent, sought to protect his property. He offered a half-pound of iron for each Red Devil hand we brought back. I and two dozen others went forth to gain wealth, but we achieved nothing. The Devils ignore arrows, and each is worth ten men in a close fight, and so we returned to Shagfe without trophies. I rode east to Shillinsk for the Varsk conclave, and saw nothing of the great battle in which the Red Devils were destroyed.'

Ifness asked in a voice of mild interest: 'Am I to understand that the Hulka defeated the Red Devils? How is this possible, if each Devil is worth ten men?'

Gulsh spat into the flames but made no reply. Srenka leaned forward to push a stick into the coals, the ring in his nose flickering with orange reflections. 'It is said that magic weapons were used.'

'By the Hulka? Where would they get magic weapons?'

'The warriors who destroyed the Red Devils were not Hulka.'

'Indeed. Who were they then?'

'I know nothing of the matter; I was at Shillinsk.'

Ifness pursued the subject no further. Etzwane rose to his feet, and climbing to the top of the rise, looked around the horizon. He saw only darkness. He listened, but could hear no sound. The night was fine; there seemed no threat from chumpa or bad ahulphs. The two Sorukhs were another matter. The same thought had occurred to Ifness, who now went to kneel before the fire. He blew up a blaze, then holding his hands to either side, made the flames jump back and forth while the Sorukhs stared in amazement. 'What are you doing?' asked Gulshe in awe.

'A trifle of magic, for my protection. I laid a command upon the fire spirit to enter the liver of all who wish me harm and there abide.'

Srenka pulled at his nose ring. 'Are you a true magician?'

Ifness laughed. 'Do you doubt it? Hold out your hand.'

Srenka cautiously extended his arm. Ifness pointed his finger and a crackling blue spark leapt to Srenka's hand. Srenka emitted a ridiculous falsetto squawk of astonishment and jerked back speechless. Gulshe sprang erect and hurriedly retreated from the fire.

'That is nothing,' said Ifness. 'Only a trifle. You are still alive, are you not? So then, we will sleep securely, all of us, knowing that magic guards us from harm.'

Etzwane spread his blanket and bedded himself down.

After a mutter or two Gulshe and Srenka arranged their own gear somewhat off to the side, near the tethered pacers. Ifness was more deliberate and sat for half an hour staring into the dying fire. At last he took himself to his own bed. For half an hour Etzwane watched the glitter of Gulshe's and Srenka's eyes from the shadow of their hoods; then he dozed and slept.

The second day was like the first. In the middle afternoon of the third day the foothills of the Kuzi Kaza came down to meet the plain. Gulshe and Srenka took counsel and established landmarks for themselves. By nightfall they had reached a desolate upland region of limestone cliffs and pinnacles. Camp was made beside a great sinkhole of dark mirror-smooth water. 'We are now in the Hulka land,' Gulshe told Ifness. 'If we are set upon, our best safety is flight, in four different directions – unless by magic you are able to insure our defense.'

'We will act as circumstances direct,' said Ifness. 'Where are the Red Devil bones?'

'Not far distant: beyond the ridge. Can you not sense the presence of so much death?'

Ifness responded in a measured voice: 'An intellect in full control of itself unfortunately must sacrifice that receptivity which distinguishes the primitive mentality. This is an evolutionary step I have, on the whole, been happy to make.'

Srenka tugged at his nose ring, uncertain whether or not Ifness had spoken in disparagement. He looked at Gulshe; they gave each other shrugs of perplexity, then went to their beds, where they muttered together for half an hour. Srenka seemed to be urging some action which Gulshe resisted; Srenka grumbled raucously; Gulshe made an ameliorative statement and both fell silent.

Etzwane sought his own blankets, where he lay wakeful, uneasy for reasons beyond his understanding. 'Perhaps,' he told himself, 'my mentality is primitive and credulous.'

During the night he awoke often to lie listening, and once heard the bickering of distant ahulphs. Another time a far mellifluous hooting reverberated through the stone defiles, to send eerie shudders along Etzwane's skin; it was a sound he could not identify. He had no awareness of returning to sleep, but when he awoke next, the sky glowed lavender to the approach of the three suns.

After a glum breakfast of dried fruit and tea, the four set forth again, passing through a series of limestone defiles, then out upon a high meadow. They rode through a forest of gallows trees, then up a barren valley. A five hundred foot crag loomed above them, with the parapets of a ruined castle at the crest. Gulshe and Srenka halted to consider the trail ahead. 'Is the castle inhabited?'

'Who knows?' growled Gulshe. 'Enough such places exist, with rogues and murderers waiting to roll down a rock, that the traveler must take care.'

Srenka pointed a crooked finger. 'Lyre birds fly above the stones; the way may be considered safe.'

'How far now to the battlefield?' asked Ifness.

'An hour's ride, around the root of yonder mountain... Come now; at a fast pace. Lyre birds or not, I mistrust these old bandit dens.'

The four rode forward at a smart gait, but the ruined castle offered no menace and the lyre birds soared as before.

They rode down from the pass. Gulshe pointed towards the great mountain, hunching like a sullen beast over the plain below. 'Thence the Red Devils came, on their way to Shagfe – there, to the north, you can barely see the Shagfe stockade. Early in the morning the men attacked, from positions they had taken during the night, and the

Red Devils were encircled. The battle lasted two hours, and all the Red Devils, with their captive women and imps, were dead; and the band which had destroyed them marched south and was seen no more: a great mystery... There! The place where the Red Devils camped. The battle raged in this vicinity. Ah! Smell the carrion!'

'What of the bones?' enquired Srenka with a sly grin. 'Do they meet your expectations?'

Ifness rode forward, across the scene of carnage. Roguskhoi corpses lay everywhere, in a clutter of twisted limbs and contorted postures. Decomposition was far advanced; ahulphs had toyed with the idea of devouring the black flesh and some had died from the experiment; these lay curled in furry balls down the slope.

Ifness rode in a great circle, gazing intently down at the corpses, sometimes halting to study one or another of the stinking red shapes at length. Etzwane halted his pacer somewhat to the side, where he could watch the Sorukhs. Ifness rode up and halted beside Etzwane. 'What do you make of the situation?'

'Like yourself, I am puzzled,' said Etzwane.

Ifness looked sidewise, eyebrows disapprovingly high. 'Why then am I puzzled?'

'Because of the wounds, which are not those of swords or cudgels.'

'Hmmf. What else have you noticed?'

Etzwane pointed. 'He with chain bib yonder appears to be a chieftain. He has suffered damage to his chest. The asutra he carried was destroyed. I noticed another dead chieftain across the field with a similar wound. The men who killed the Roguskhoi, like ourselves, knew of the asutra.'

Ifness gave a curt nod of the head. 'So it would seem.'

The Sorukh approached, wearing artificial smiles. 'The

bones then,' Srenka put forward, 'what of all these fine bones?'

'They are obviously not in salable condition,' said Ifness. 'I can make no firm offer until you clean and dry them, make up standard bales, and convey them to the Shillinsk dock.'

Gulshe gave his flowing mustache a sad tug; Srenka was less controlled. 'I feared such duplicity!' he cried. 'We have no guarantee of profit; we have invested time and property to no avail, and I for one will not let the matter rest on these terms.'

Ifness said coldly, 'Upon our return to Shillinsk I will compensate you and your comrade generously; as you point out, you have done your best. However, I cannot undertake to buy a field full of corpses in order to gratify your avarice. You must find another customer.'

Srenka twisted his face into a ferocious grimace, his lower canine tusks gripping his nose ring. Gulshe warned him with a gesture. 'The protests are reasonable. Our friend understandably cannot burden himself with merchandise in its present condition. I am certain that a mutually profitable arrangement is possible. In a year the bones will be well weathered and in prime condition, or we might rent slaves to boil and strip the carcasses. In the meantime let us leave this foul place; I feel a presentiment.'

'To Shagfe then,' growled Srenka. 'At Shagfe I plan to drink a crock of Baba's cellar brew.'

'A moment,' said Ifness, scrutinising the hillside. 'I am interested in the band which destroyed the Red Devils. Where did they go after the victory?'

'Back the way they had come,' sneered Srenka. 'Where else?'

'They did not visit Shagfe?'

'At Shagfe you can make your own enquiries.'

Etzwane said, 'Ahulphs might track them.'

'They are a month gone and far away,' said Ifness. 'The effort might well be tedious.'

'In Shagfe we will undoubtedly hear news,' suggested Gulshe.

'To Shagfe then,' said Srenka. 'I thirst for old Baba's cellar brew.'

Ifness turned a reflective glance towards Shagfe. Gulshe and Srenka already were riding down the long slope. They halted and looked back. 'Come along then; the day will not last forever; yonder is Shagfe!'

'Very well,' said Ifness. 'We will visit Shagfe.'

Shagfe, a dreary and unprepossessing settlement, baked in the lavender sunlight. Rude mud huts straggled along a wind-scoured street; behind was a scatter of leather tents. A rambling flat-roofed structure of mud and wattle dominated the town: the inn and grog shop. A clattering windmill near by drew water into a tank, which overflowed into a trough; here sat a band of ahulphs who had come to drink. They had brought rock crystals and already had bartered for rags of yellow cloth, which they wore rakishly tied to their hearing knobs.

Riding into Shagfe the four passed the slave pens: a complex of three sheds and three fenced yards in which a score of men, as many women, and several dozen blank-eyed children were confined.

Ifness, drawing his pacer to a halt, turned to Gulshe. 'Who are these captives, local persons?'

Gulshe examined the group without interest. 'They appear to be strangers, probably excess folk sold by the hetman of their clan. They might be persons taken in raids beyond the mountains. Or they might be persons seized and sold by private enterprises.' Gulshe gave a curious choked chuckle. 'In short, they are anyone unable to prevent otherwise. Here there is no one to say us nay, and each man must see to his own welfare.'

'Such an existence is unpleasant,' said Etzwane in disgust.

Gulshe looked at him without comprehension and turned to Ifness as if questioning Etzwane's sanity; Ifness smiled grimly. 'Who buys the slaves?'

Gulshe shrugged. 'Hozman Sore-throat takes them all, and pays a good weight of metal in the bargain.'

'You are very knowledgeable in this regard,' said Etzwane in a dour voice.

Srenka said, 'And what of that? Do you begrudge us a livelihood? Perhaps the time has come for an understanding.'

'Yes,' said Gulshe, 'the time has come.' He brought forth a heavy-bladed knife of polished black glass. 'Magic is not proof against my knife, and I can split either of you as if you were melons. Dismount from the pacers and stand facing the pens.'

Ifness asked in a mild voice, 'Am I to understand that you intend us an inconvenience?'

'We are men of trade,' Srenka declared in a boisterous voice. 'We live for profit. If we cannot sell bones, we will sell slaves, and for this reason we have brought you to Shagfe. I likewise am adept with the throwing-knife. Dismount!'

'It is humiliating to be captured directly in front of the slave pens,' said Ifness. 'You show no regard for our sensibilities, and if for this reason alone, we refuse to gratify your wishes.'

Srenka guffawed. Gulshe allowed a yellow line of teeth to show below his mustache. 'Dismount; to the ground, and promptly!'

Etzwane spoke softly, 'Have you forgotten the curse imposed at Shillinsk?'

'Hundreds of curses already ride our backs; what harm is another?' Gulshe jerked his knife. 'Dismount.'

Ifness shrugged. 'Well, then, if we must, we must . . . Destiny plays strange tricks.' Alighting wearily, he placed his hand on the pacer's haunch. The pacer roared in pain and sprang forward, into Gulshe's pacer, toppling the beast to the ground. Srenka flung his knife at Etzwane, who had dropped to the ground; the knife cut the air a foot over his shoulder. Ifness reached up, grasped Srenka's nose-ring. Srenka emitted a quivering hiss, which would have been a scream had he been able to articulate. 'Hold him by the ring,' Ifness instructed Etzwane. 'Keep him in a state of compliance.' Ifness went to where Gulshe, scrambling, cursing, clawing at the ground, attempted to gain his feet. Ifness laid a comradely hand on Gulshe's shoulder; Gulshe gave a spasmodic jerk and fell once more to the ground. 'I fear I must take your knife,' said Ifness. 'You will not need it again.'

Etzwane and Ifness continued towards the mud-and-wattle inn, leading the riderless beasts. Ifness said, 'Six ounces of silver for two able individuals; it seems no great sum. Perhaps we were gulled. But no matter, in any event. Gulshe and Srenka will profit greatly by learning another facet of the slavery trade . . . I could almost wish that . . . but no! It is uncharitable to think of my colleague Dasconetta in this connection. Almost I regret the parting of ways with Gulshe and Srenka. They were picturesque companions.'

Etzwane looked back over his shoulder to the slave pens. Except for Ifness' energy pack, he would now be peering forth from between the withes. Still – these were the risks he had weighed in Garwiy; he had elected to face them rather than pursue a life of security, music and ease . . . Ifness was speaking, as much to himself as to Etzwane:

'I regret only that we failed to learn more from Gulshe and Srenka . . . Well, here we are at the hostelry. In retrospect the inn at Shillinsk seems a haven of palatial luxury. We will represent ourselves not as wizards nor research students, nor even bone merchants. The most prestigious occupation at Shagfe is slavery, and slavery is our trade.'

At the inn they paused to survey the settlement. The afternoon was warm and placid: infants crawled in the dirt; older children played at slave-taking among the tents, leaping forth with ropes to drag away their captives. At the trough under the windmill three squat dark-haired women in leather pants and straw capes bickered with the ahulphs. The women carried sticks and struck at the ahulphs' long sensitive feet whenever they attempted to drink: the ahulphs in turn kicked dirt at the women and screamed abuse. Beside the road a dozen crones in shapeless straw cloaks huddled beside offerings of goods to be traded: mounds of dark-red meal, thongs of dried meat, blue-black finger grubs in boxes of wet moss, fat greenbeetles tethered to stakes, sugar pods, boiled birds, cardamoms, salt crusts. Above, the vast bright sky; to all sides, the hot flat plain; far in the east a band of riders, visible only as a vibration of black specks, with a thin plume of lavender dust above . . . Ifness and Etzwane approached the inn, and entered by a hole in the mud wall. The common room was dim and dank-smelling. A rack behind the counter supported three barrels; elsewhere were benches and stools where half a dozen men sat with earthenware bowls of sour seed wine or mugs of the famous Shagfe cellar brew. Conversation halted; the men stared at Ifness and Etzwane with a still intensity. The sole illumination was the purple glare of outdoors seeping through the door-hole. Ifness and Etzwane peered around the room while their eyes adjusted to the dimness.

A short, bare-chested man with long white hair ambled

forward. He wore a leather apron and knee boots, and was apparently Baba the proprietor. He inquired their needs in a rough dialect which Etzwane understood more through divination than comprehension.

Ifness responded in a fair simulation of the dialect. 'What sort of lodging are you able to provide us?'

'The best to be had in Shagfe,' declared Baba the innkeeper. 'Anyone will tell you as much. Is your question motivated by sheer curiosity?'

'No,' replied Ifness. 'You may show us the best you have to offer.'

'That is simple enough,' said Baba. 'This way, if you please.' He led them down an ill-smelling corridor, past a rudimentary kitchen where a great kettle of porridge simmered over a fire, and into a bare courtyard, sheltered around the periphery by an overhanging roof. 'Select whatever area you wish. The rain generally sweeps in from the south and the south bay is the driest.'

Ifness nodded gravely. 'The lodging is adequate. What of our pacers?'

'I will take them to my stable and feed them hay, provided that you make suitable recompense. How long is your stay?'

'A day or two, or even longer, depending upon the transaction of our business. We are slave traders with a commission to buy a dozen stout Red Devils to row the galley of an east coast potentate. We understand, however, that the Red Devils have all been killed, which is sad news to hear.'

'Your misfortune is my great luck, for they were on the march towards Shagfe and might well have destroyed my hostelry.'

'Perhaps the conquerors took captives?'

'I believe not, but in the common room sits Fabrache the Lucky Little Survivor. He claims to have witnessed the battle, and who is to doubt his word? If you were to provide a mug or two of cellar brew, his tongue would wag freely, I vouch for this.'

'A happy thought. Now, as to the fee for shelter and food, for us and our pacers . . .'

The haggling proceeded, Ifness driving a hard bargain in order to avoid a reputation for openhandedness. After five minutes a value defined as two ounces of silver was placed upon high-quality food and lodging for a period of five days.

'Very good then,' said Ifness, 'though as usual I have allowed a skillful rhetorician to persuade me into foolish extravagance. Let us now confer with Fabrache the Lucky Little Survivor. How did he gain this unusual cognomen?'

'It is no more than a child's pet name. Three times as an infant his mother attempted to drown him, and each time he pushed up through the mud. She gave up her task in disgust, and even bestowed the diminutive upon him. He became a man without fear; he reasonably argues that if Gaspard the God desired his death, he would not have overlooked this early opportunity . . .'

Baba led the way back to the common room. He called, 'I introduce to the company the noble Ifness and Etzwane, who have come to Shagfe to buy slaves.'

A man to the side gave a dispirited moan. 'So now they compete with Hozman Sore-throat to drive prices still higher?'

'Hozman Sore-throat has bid for no Red Devils, which these traders require.' Baba the innkeeper turned to a tall, thin man with a long, dismal face and a beard hanging below his chin like an icicle of black hair. 'Fabrache, what are the facts? How many Red Devils still survive?'

Fabrache responded with the deliberation of an obstinate man. 'The Red Devils are extinct in the Mirkil district, which is to say, in the neighborhood of Shagfe. I spoke with men of the Tchark race from south of the Kuzi Kaza; they reported that the Red Devil bands had joined into a single horde, which then had marched north. Two days later I watched an army of magicians destroy this horde. Each Red Devil was killed and then rekilled: an astounding sight which I will never forget.'

'The magic army took no captives?' asked Ifness.

'None. They destroyed the Red Devils and marched away into the east. I descended to the battlefield to salvage metal, but ahulphs had preceded me and every ounce was preempted. But this is not all my tale. As I turned towards Shagfe I saw a great ship lift into the air, light as fluff, and disappear behind the clouds.'

'A miraculous vision!' declared Ifness. 'Inkeeper, supply this man a mug of cellar brew.'

Etzwane asked, 'Was the ship round as a disk and the color of copper-bronze?'

Fabrache the Lucky Little Survivor made a negative sign. 'This was an impressive black globe. The copper disks you mention were seen at the great battle of spaceships; the disks and the black globes fought together.'

Ifness nodded gravely and darted a warning glance towards Etzwane. 'We have heard something of this battle. Eight copper ships engaged six black globes at a place whose name I forget.'

The others in the room hastened to contradict him. 'Your information is inaccurate. Four of the black globes attacked two of the copper disks, and the copper ships were broken into fragments.'

'I wonder if we refer to the same battle,' Ifness mused. 'When did your affair occur?'

'Only two days ago; we have spoken of little else since. Such events have never before occurred in the Mirkil district.'

'Where did this battle take place?' asked Ifness.

'Over yonder in the Orgai Mountains,' said Fabrache. 'Behind Thrie Orgai, or so it is said; I have not been there myself.'

'Think of it, so close to Shagfe!' exclaimed Baba the innkeeper. 'Hardly two days' ride on a sound pacer!'

'We are traveling in that direction,' said Ifness. 'I would like to inspect the locality.' He addressed the Lucky Little Survivor. 'Would you care to act as our guide?'

Fabrache tugged at his beard. He glanced aside at one of his fellows. 'What is the news of the Gogursk clan? Have they made their west-faring?'

'No fear for the Gogursks,' said his friend. 'This year they drive south to Lake Urman for crabs. The Orgai is empty of threat, except naturally for the predations of Hozman Sore-throat.'

From outside the inn sounded a thud of hooves, the creaking of leather, hoarse voices. The landlord looked out through the doorway and spoke over his shoulder, 'Kash Blue-worms.'

At this two of the men present rose quickly and departed by the back corridor. Another called out, 'Fabrache, what of you? Did you not take four Blue-worm girls to Hozman?'

'I am not one to discuss my business in public,' said the Lucky Little Survivor. 'In any case, the incident occurred last year.'

The tribesmen entered the room. After glaring through the dimness they strode to tables and rapped on the planks for drink. They were nine in number, burly, moon-faced men with fringe beards, wearing limp leather trousers, black boots studded with flint cabochons, blouses of faded green jute, headgear of dry seed pods sewed into the shape of a pointed casque; these rattled with each motion of the head. Etzwane thought them the most ruffianly band of his experience, and leaned back from the unpleasant odors that had accompanied them into the room.

The oldest of the Kash gave his head-rattles a shake, and called out in a roaring voice, 'Where is the man who buys slaves at high prices?'

Fabrache responded in a subdued voice, 'He is not present.'

Baba the innkeeper asked cautiously, 'You have slaves to sell?'

'We do indeed, consisting of those persons now present, save only the innkeeper. Please consider yourselves our captives.'

Fabrache uttered a cry of indignation. 'This is not customary procedure! A man is entitled to drink beer at Shagfe in security!'

'Additionally,' Baba declared, 'I will tolerate no such conduct. What would happen to my custom? You must retract your threat.'

The old Kash grinned and rattle his seed pods. 'Very well; in view of the general protest we will put our best interests to the side. Still, we must have a word with Hozman Sore-throat. He has treated the Kash clan with severity; where does he sell so many of our folk?'

'Others have put similar questions, but received no answer,' said Baba. 'Hozman Sore-throat is not now in Shagfe, and I know nothing of his plans.'

The old Blue-worm made a gesture of resignation. 'In that case we will drink your cellar brew and make a meal of your cooked food, the odor of which I detect.'

'All very well, and how will you pay?'

'We carry with us sacks of safad oil, to settle our score.'

Baba said, 'Bring in the oil, while I work the scum off a new cask of cellar brew.'

The evening passed without bloodshed. Ifness and Etzwane sat to the side watching the burly figures lurch back and forth across the firelight. Etzwane tried to define the way in which these roaring celebrants differed from the general population of Shant: intensity, gusto, a focus of every faculty upon the immediate instant – such qualities characterised the folk of Caraz. Trivial acts induced exaggerated reactions. Laughter racked the ribs; rage came fierce and sudden; woe was so intense as to be intolerable. Upon every aspect of existence the clansmen fixed a keen and minute perception, allowing nothing to go unnoticed. Such raptures and transports of emotion left little time for meditation, Etzwane mused. How could a Blue-worm Hulka become a musician when he suffered a congenital lack of patience? Wild dancing around the campfire, mêlées, and murders – this was more the barbarian style . . . Etzwane and Ifness presently departed the company. They unrolled their blankets under the overhang of the courtyard and lay down to rest. For a period Etzwane lay listening to the muffled revels from the common room. He wanted to ask Ifness his theories regarding the battle between spaceships which had occurred behind Thrie Orgai, but had no stomach for a caustic or ambiguous reply . . . If the asutra and their hosts had manned the copper disks, what race had built black space-globes? For that matter, what race of men with magic weapons had destroyed the Roguskhoi? Why had men, Roguskhoi, copper and black spaceships all come to Caraz to do battle? . . . Etzwane put a cautious question to Ifness, 'Do any of the Earth worlds build space-vessels in the shape of black globes?'

The question was succinct and precise; Ifness could find no fault with it. He answered in an even voice, 'To my knowledge, no.' And he added, 'I am as puzzled as yourself. It would appear that the asutra have enemies somewhere among the stars. Perhaps human enemies.'

'This possibility alone justifies your defiance of Dasconetta,' declared Etzwane.

'So it might seem.'

The Kash Blue-worms chose to sleep in the open beside their pacers; Etzwane and Ifness passed a tranquil night.

In the cool mauve morning Baba brought them mugs of hot cellar brew with floating dollops of the sour local cheese. 'If you fare towards Thrie Orgai, depart early. You will cross the Wild Waste by midafternoon, and can spend the night in a tree along the Vurush.'

'Good advice,' said Ifness. 'Prepare us a breakfast of fried meat and bread, and send a boy to arouse Fabrache. Additionally, we will drink herbal tea with our meal, rather than this excellent but overnutritious brew.'

'Fabrache is on hand,' said the innkeeper. 'He wants to leave while the Blue-worms are still torpid. Your breakfast is already prepared. It consists of porridge and locust paste, like everyone else's. As for the tea, I can boil up a broth of pepperweed, if this suits your taste.'

Ifness gave a resigned acquiescence. 'Bring our pacers around to the front; we depart as soon as possible.'

Chapter 5

The Kash Blue-worms were stirring when Ifness, Etzwane, and Fabrache rode forth. One man growled a malediction; another half rose to look after them; but they were in no mood for exertion.

From Shagfe the three rode west across the Wild Waste, an alkali flat stretching out to the limits of vision. The surface was a hard bone-white crust, powdered with a soft, acrid dust. Across the waste marched a dozen wind-devils, back and forth like dancers of a pavane, out to the horizon and back again, some tall and stately against the brilliant sky, others low to the ground, scurrying without dignity, presently collapsing into purposeless puffs and wisps. For a period Fabrache kept a watch to the rear, but when the huddle of huts disappeared into the dusty lavender distance and no bounding black shapes came in pursuit, he showed a somewhat more confident disposition. Looking sidewise towards Ifness, he spoke in a cautious voice, 'Last night we struck no formal contract, but I assume that we travel in confederacy and that neither party will attempt subjugation of the other.'

Ifness endorsed this point of view. 'We have no particular interest in slavery,' said Ifness. 'We sold a pair of prime Sorukhs on our way into Shagfe, but to speak frankly, the life of a slaver is too precarious and unrewarding, at least in the Mirkil district.'

'The region is over exploited,' said Fabrache. 'Since Hozman Sore-throat became active the population has diminished by a half. At Shagfe Inn we would see many strange faces, many different costumes and styles. Each Hulka clan maintained from three to seven fetish groups; then there would be Sorukhs from Shillinsk district, Shovel-heads and Alulas from Lake Nior, folk from over the Kuzi Kaza. A small slaver such as myself could earn a modest livelihood and keep a girl or two for his own use. Hozman Sore-throat has put an end to all this. Now we must scour the countryside for sheer sustenance.'

'Where does Hozman Sore-throat market his merchandise?'

'Hozman keeps good secrets,' said Fabrache with a spiteful sniff. 'Someday he will go too far. The world is going sour; it was not thus when I was a boy. Think of it! Spaceships in battle; Red Devils looting and killing; Hozman Sore-throat and his illusory boon of inflationary prices. Then when he destroys us and depopulates Mirkil district, he will move on and work the same outrage elsewhere.'

'I look forward to meeting Hozman,' said Ifness. 'He must have interesting tales to tell.'

'To the contrary; he is as terse as a costive chumpa.'

'We shall see, we shall see.'

As the day progressed, the air quieted and the wind-devils disappeared; the three crossed the flat with no discomfort other than the baking heat. By midafternoon the first slopes of the Orgai bulked ahead and the Wild Waste lay behind. As the three suns dropped behind the mountains, they rode over a hill and saw before them the broad Vurush, flowing from behind the Thrie Orgai and north into the haze. A grove of gnarled yews grew down to the water's edge, and here Fabrache chose to camp for the night, though chumpa traces were evident along the shore.

'They cannot be avoided, no matter where we camp,' said Fabrache. 'Three men with firebrands can keep them at a distance, if such a need arises.'

'Then we must keep watch during the night?'

'Not at all,' replied Fabrache. 'The pacers will watch, and I will keep the fire ablaze.'

He tethered the pacers to a tree and built a fire on the shore. Then, while Ifness and Etzwane collected a stack of resinous yew branches, Fabrache snared a dozen mud crabs, which he cracked, cleaned, and toasted, and meanwhile cooked meal cakes on hot, flat stones. 'You are highly efficient,' said Ifness. 'It is a pleasure to watch you at work.'

Fabrache gave his head a dour shake. 'I know nothing else but this; a skill acquired across a lifetime of hardship. I take no great pleasure from your compliment.'

'Surely you have other skills?'

'Yes. I am reckoned a good barber. Occasionally in jest I imitate the mating antics of the ahulphs. But these are modest accomplishments; ten years after my death I will be forgotten, and one with the soil of Caraz. Still, I consider myself a fortunate man, more so than most. I have often wondered why it was given to me to live the life of Kyril Fabrache.'

'These reflections, at one time or another, have occurred to all of us,' said Ifness, 'but unless we are agreed upon a religion of gradated reincarnation, the question is ingenuous.' He rose to his feet and surveyed the landscape. 'I assume that the Red Devils never ranged this far west?'

Piqued by Ifness' indifference to his quest for personal truth, Fabrache gave only a short reply. 'They never even reached Shagfe.' He went off to tend the pacers.

Ifness considered the mass of the Orgai to the north, where the crag Thrie Orgai flared purple in the last rays of the setting suns. 'In this case, the spaceship battle would seem isolated from the slaughter of the Roguskhoi,' he mused. 'The events are of course related; there can be no doubt of this much . . . Tomorrow will be an interesting day.' He made one of his rare gesticulations. 'If I can produce a spaceship, even a hulk, I am vindicated. Dasconetta will be gray with rage; even now he gnaws his knuckles by the hour . . . We can only hope that these spaceships exist in fact, that they are something more than mare's nests.'

Etzwane, vaguely irked by the nature of Ifness' aspirations, said, 'I can see no value to a wrecked spaceship; they have been known for thousands of years, and must be common throughout the system of Earth worlds.'

'True,' declared Ifness, still elevated by his visions of triumph, 'but these are the product of human knowledge, and many knowledges exist.'

'Bah,' growled Etzwane. 'Iron is iron, glass is glass, and this is the same here or at the end of the universe.'

'True once more. The gross elementals are known to all. But there is no finite limit to knowledge. Each set of apparent ultimates is susceptible to examination and must be analysed in new terms. These succeeding layers of knowledge are numberless. Those familiar to us are each derived from the level above, or below. Conceivably entire disassociated phases of knowledge exist; the field of parapsychology comes to mind. The basic law of the cosmos is this: in a situation of infinity, whatever is possible exists in fact. To particularise, the technology which propels an alien spaceship may be different from that of Earth, and such a technology must be a matter of intense interest, if only philosophically.' Ifness considered the fire. 'I must remark that augmented knowledge is not necessarily a boon, and might easily be dangerous.'

'In that case,' Etzwane asked, 'why are you so anxious to broadcast this knowledge?'

Ifness chuckled. 'First, it is my normal human inclination to do so. Second, the group of which I am part – from which Dasconetta would naturally be expelled – is competent to control the most dangerous secrets. Thirdly, I cannot overlook my personal advantage. If I deliver an alien spaceship to the Historical Institute, even a wrecked hulk, I will gain great prestige.'

Etzwane turned away to make up his bed, reflecting that of Ifness' three reasons, the last was probably the most cogent.'

The night passed without incident. Three times Etzwane awoke. Once he heard from far off the rumbling challenge of a chumpa and from an even greater distance the answering calls of an ahulph tribe, but none came to disturb the camp by the river.

Fabrache awoke before dawn. Blowing up the fire, he prepared a breakfast of porridge boiled with pepper meat and tea.

Not long after dawn the three mounted their pacers and set off to the south along the banks of the Vurush. Gradually they rose into the Orgai.

Shortly before noon Fabrache jerked his pacer to a halt. He cocked his head as if listening, and looked slowly to all sides.

'What is the matter?' asked Ifness.

Fabrache said nothing. He pointed ahead towards the gap into a stony valley. 'Here is where the black globes discovered the disk ships; here is where the battle took place.' Rising to stand in his stirrups he searched the hillsides and reexamined the sky.

'You have a presentiment,' said Etzwane softly.

Fabrache pulled nervously at his beard. 'The valley has

known a wonderful event; the air still tingles . . . Is there not something more?' Fretfully he swung his gaunt body around in the saddle, rolling his eyes from side to side. 'There is pressure upon me.'

Etzwane scanned the valley. To right and left, harsh gullies cut into sandstone, the high areas baking white-violet in the sunlight, the deep shadows a black bottle-green. A flicker of motion caught his eye; not a hundred feet distant crouched a large ahulph, considering whether or not to hurl a stone. Etzwane said, 'Perhaps you feel the gaze of yonder ahulph.'

Fabrache swung about, annoyed that Etzwane had seen the creature first. The ahulph, a blue-black buck of a variety unknown to Etzwane, shook its ear fibers uneasily and started to move away. Fabrache called out in de-da pidgin. The ahulph paused. Fabrache spoke again, and with the swaggering waggishness typical of the higher ahulphs, it bounded down from the jut. Politely it released a waft of 'gregariousness'* and sidled forward. Fabrache dismounted from his pacer and signaled Etzwane and Ifness to do likewise. Tossing a chunk of cold grain cake to the ahulph, he spoke again in de-da. The ahulph made a fervent and elaborate response.

Fabrache turned to Ifness and Etzwane. 'The ahulph watched the battle. He has explained to me the sequence of events. Two copper disk-ships landed at the end of the valley and remained there almost a week. Persons came out to walk around. They stood on two feet, but exuded a

* The higher ahulphs control four odors, signifying gregariousness, hostility, and two varieties of excitement unknown to the human race. The innumerable races of lower ahulphs vent only hostility and an attractive scent. The ahulph mentality at times seems to resemble human intelligence, but the similarity is misleading, and attempts to deal with ahulphs on a basis of human rationality end in frustration. The ahulph, for instance, cannot understand working for hire, no matter how carefully the matter is explained.

nonhuman odor. The ahulph paid no attention to their appearance. They did nothing during their stay and came outside only at dawn and dusk. Three days ago, at noon, four black globes appeared a mile overhead. The disk-ships were taken by surprise. The black globes sent down lightning bolts and exploded both disk-ships, then departed as abruptly as they had come. The ahulphs watched the wrecks, but felt diffident about approaching. Yesterday a large disk-ship dropped from the sky. After hovering an hour, it lifted the hulk which had suffered the least damage and carried it away. Fragments of the second hulk remain.'

'Interesting news,' murmured Ifness. 'Toss the creature another morsel of grain cake. I am anxious to inspect the shattered hulk.'

Fabrache scratched his chin where the first hairs of his beard had their roots. 'I must admit to a diffidence not unlike that of the ahulph. The valley holds an uncanny presence which I do not care to test.'

'Do not apologise,' said Ifness. 'You are not known as the Lucky Little Survivor for nothing. Will you await us here, in company with the ahulph?'

'This I will do,' said Fabrache.

Ifness and Etzwane set off up the valley. They rode a mile, the sandstone rising to either side in crags and juts. The valley floor widened to become a sandy flat, and here they found the hulk of the second ship. The outer skin had been rent and torn in a dozen places; one entire section had disappeared. From the gaps spewed tangled metal and viscous oozes. The top surface had been exploded into tatters, which lay scattered across the plain; the ground below showed rings of white, green, and yellow powder.

Ifness gave a hiss of vexation. He snatched out his camera and photographed the hulk. 'I had expected nothing better than this; still I had hoped. What a trophy had the ship been susceptible to study! A new cosmology, in effect, to compare with our own! A tragedy to find it thus!'

Etzwane felt mildly surprised at Ifness' vehemence: such a display was unusual. They moved closer and the wrecked spaceship exerted an eerie fascination, a strange, sad majesty. Ifness alighted from his pacer. He picked up a fragment of metal, hefted it, cast it aside. He went up to the hulk, peered into the interior, shook his head in disgust. 'Everything of interest is either vaporised, crushed, or melted; we have nothing to learn here.'

Etzwane spoke. 'You notice that a segment of the ship is missing? Look yonder in that gulch: there it has lodged.'

Ifness looked where Etzwane had directed. 'The ship was attacked first, perhaps, by a burst of explosive force, and then struck again, with energy sufficient to cause the melting.' He set off towards the gulch, about fifty yards distant, into which a pie-shaped section of the ship had wedged itself. The outer skin, dented and distorted but by some miracle untorn, had plastered itself across the narrow opening like a great bronze seal.

The two scrambled up the stones until they could step over to the crumpled metal. Ifness tugged at the edge of a fractured section. Etzwane joined him; by dint of straining the two bent aside the sheet to provide an opening into the hull. A vile odor issued forth: a stench of decay, different from any Etzwane had known before . . . He became rigid, held up his hand. 'Listen.'

From below came a faint scraping sound, persisting two or three seconds.

'Something seems to be alive,' Etzwane peered down into the dark. The prospect of entering the broken ship had no appeal for him.

Ifness had no such qualms. From his pouch he brought an object which Etzwane had never seen before: a transparent cube half an inch on a side. Suddenly it emitted a flood of light, which Ifness turned into the dim interior. Four feet below a broken bench slanted across what seemed to be a storage chamber; a clutter of objects flung from racks lay mounded against the far wall. Ifness stepped down upon the bench and jumped to the floor. Etzwane took a last wistful look around the valley and followed. Ifness stood surveying the heaped articles against the wall. He pointed. 'A corpse.' Etzwane moved to where he could see. The dead creature lay on its back, pressed against the wall. 'An anthropomorphic biped,' said Ifness. 'Distinctly not a man; not even manlike, except for two legs, two arms, and a head. It even smells different from human carrion.'

'Worse,' muttered Etzwane. He bent forward, studying the dead thing, which wore no garments save various straps for the support of three pouches, one at either hip, one at the back of the head. The skin, a purplish-black parchment, seemed as hard as old leather. The head displayed a number of parallel bony ridges, originating at the top of a protective ring around the single eye and running back across the scalp. A mouth-like orifice appeared at the base of the neck. Pads of matted bristle conceivably served as auditory organs.

Ifness saw something which had escaped Etzwane. He reached for a tubular rod, then lunged forward and thrust. In the shadows at the back of the dead creature's neck was a stir of sudden movement, but Ifness was too quick; the rod struck into a small dark object. Ifness pried the body away from the wall, struck again at the small six-legged creature who had ridden in the pouch at the back of the dead neck.

'Asutra?' asked Etzwane.

Ifness gave his head a jerk of assent. 'Asutra and host.'

Etzwane inspected the two-legged creature once more.

'It is something like the Roguskhoi in the hard skin, the shape of the head, the hands and feet.'

'I noted the similarity,' said Ifness. 'It might be a collateral form, or the stock from which the Roguskhoi derived.' He spoke tonelessly; his eyes darted this way and that. Etzwane had never seen him so keen. 'Quietly now,' said Ifness.

On long, soft steps he went to the bulkhead and turned his light through an aperture.

They looked along a hall twenty feet long, the bulkheads twisted and distorted. Into the far end seeped a wan daylight, filtering through overhead fractures.

Ifness strode quietly down the hall into the terminating room, holding the light-cube in one hand, an energy gun in the other.

The room was vacant. Etzwane could not imagine its function or purpose. A bench flanked three walls, with cabinets above containing objects of glass and metal to which Etzwane could put no name. The outside skin and one wall pressed on to the fractured rock, which comprised the fourth wall. Ifness glared in all directions like a gaunt gray hawk. He cocked his head to listen; Etzwane did the same. The air was thick and quiet. Etzwane asked in a low voice, 'What is this room?'

Ifness gave his head a curt shake. 'They contrive things differently on Earth-world ships . . . I can understand nothing of this.'

'Look there.' Etzwane pointed. 'More asutra.' A glass tray at the end of the bench contained a murky fluid in which floated three dozen dark ellipsoids, like so many black olives. Below, indistinct in the matrix, hung still arms.

Ifness went to examine the tank. A tube entered one of the sides; from this tube filaments led up to the asutra. 'They seem cataleptic,' said Ifness. 'Perhaps they take energy, or information, or entertainment.' He stood thinking a moment, then spoke. 'We can do no more. The matter is now too large for our sole discretion, and in fact is overwhelming.' He paused to look around the chamber. 'There is material here to occupy ten thousand analysts, to astound the Institute. We will return at once to Shillinsk. From the boat I can signal Dasconetta, and through him order out a salvage ship.'

'Something aboard is yet alive,' said Etzwane. 'We cannot leave it to die.' As if to reinforce his remark, a scraping sound issued from behind the crumpled wall opposite the hall.

'A ticklish business,' muttered Ifness. 'What if twenty Roguskhoi burst out upon us? . . . On the other hand, something might be learned from a host not under asutra control. Well then, let us look. But careful and easy! We must be on guard.'

He went to the area where the wall met the rock. At the center and bottom, contact was not complete, leaving irregular openings, the diameter of a man's head, through which air could pass. Etzwane peered through the center gap. For a moment he saw nothing, then abruptly a round object the size of a large coin came into view, reflecting a nacreous pink and green shimmer. Etzwane drew back, oppressed by a thrilling of the nerves. He collected himself and spoke in a low voice. 'It is one of the host-things. I looked into its eye.'

Ifness made a curt sound. 'If it is alive, it is mortal, and there is no need for panic.'

Etzwane choked back a retort, and taking up a metal bar, began to attack the rock. Ifness stood back, an enigmatic expression on his face.

The rock, shattered by the impact of the ship, broke away in chunks. Etzwane worked with a furious energy, as if to distract himself. The center gap grew wide. Etzwane paid no heed and drove the bar furiously into the rock . . . Ifness held up his hand. 'Sufficient.' He stepped forward, flashed his light into the hole, to reveal a dark, waiting shape. 'Come forth,' said Ifness, and gestured, his hand in the illumination.

There was first silence. Then slowly, but without hesitation, the creature pulled itself through the hole. Like the corpse it stood naked but for a harness and three pouches, one of which held an asutra. Ifness spoke to Etzwane. 'Lead the way to the outside. I will direct the creature to follow you.'

Etzwane turned away. Ifness stepped forward, touched the creature's arm, pointed.

The creature stalked after Etzwane – down the hall, into the chamber which was open to the sky.

Etzwane climbed up on the bench, pushed his head up into the daylight. Never had air seemed so clear and sweet. And in the sky a mile overhead hovered a great disk-ship, slowly rotating on its vertical axis, the three suns laying three-colored reflections on the copper-bronze skin. Another mile above hung four smaller ships.

Etzwane stared up in consternation. The large disk-ship descended slowly. He called the news back down to Ifness.

'Hurry,' said Ifness. 'Help the creature up and hold fast to his harness.'

Etzwane scrambled out and stood waiting. From below rose the purple-black head, ridges of bone running across the scalp. The head protruded, and the shoulders, with the pouch containing the asutra. On sudden impulse Etzwane seized the pouch and pulled it away from the black body. A nerve cord stretched; the creature uttered a guttural gasp and released its grip on the edge of the hole, and would have fallen backward had Etzwane not clamped his arm around the corded neck. With his other hand he drew the dagger from his belt and slashed the nerve; the asutra, squirming and clutching, pulled free. Etzwane threw it to the surface of the ship, then heaved the dark creature up after it. Ifness quickly followed. 'What is the commotion?'

'I pulled the asutra loose. There it goes yonder. Hold the host; I will kill it.'

Ifness, frowning in displeasure, obeyed. The black host-creature lunged after Etzwane; Ifness clung to its harness. Etzwane ran after the scuttling black object. He picked up a stone, held it high, smashed it down upon the black bulb.

Ifness meanwhile had propelled the suddenly listless creature behind a wall of rock, screening the descending spaceship from its sight. Etzwane, leading the pacers, joined them.

Ifness asked in a frosty voice, 'Why did you kill the asutra? You have left us an empty shell, hardly worth the effort of removing.'

Etzwane said drily, 'I recognise this. I also notice the descending ship, and I have been told that the asutra communicate telepathically with their fellows. I thought to afford us a better chance of escape.'

Ifness grunted. 'The telepathic capability of the asutra has never been established.' He looked up the gulch. 'The way appears to be feasible. We must hurry, however . . . It is possible that Fabrache may think better of waiting overlong.'

Chapter 6

The gulch, narrow, tortuous, and strewn with boulders, afforded no scope for riding. Etzwane scrambled ahead, leading the pacers. Behind came the dark creature, its unearthly tendons twitching and pulling in unfamiliar sequences. At the rear strolled Ifness, cool and detached.

Once behind the ridge they veered to the south and so returned to where they had left Fabrache. They found him lolling at his ease against a rock overlooking the valley, where now no spaceships could be seen, wrecked or otherwise. Fabrache leapt to his feet with an ejaculation of shock, for they had come up on him quietly from the side. Ifness held up his hand, admonishing Fabrache to placidity and composure. 'As you see,' said Ifness, 'we have succored a survivor of the battle. Have you seen its like before?'

'Never!' declared Fabrache. 'I am not pleased to see it now. Where will you sell it? Who would care to buy such a thing?'

Ifness gave one of his rare chuckles. 'It commands value as a curiosity, if nothing else. A collector's item, so to speak. I have no doubt as to our eventual profit. But what occurred yonder in the valley?'

Fabrache stared in wonder. 'What? Did you not witness the happening at first hand?'

'We took refuge behind the hill,' Ifness explained. 'Had

we remained to watch, we ourselves might have been observed, with no telling as to the consequences.'

'Of course, of course; this is clear enough. Well, the rest of the affair surpasses my comprehension. A great ship descended and seized upon the wreck and took it up as if it were a biscuit –'

'Did they hoist one section?' Ifness demanded, 'Or two?'

'Two. The ship swooped a second time, and I thought, alas! what a sad end for my slaving companions! Then, as I sat there reflecting upon the remarkable life which it has been my good fortune to live, you crept up and found me musing. Aha!' Fabrache shook his head in mournful self-reproach. 'Had you been Hozman Sore-throat, my time as a free man would now be done. What now is our program?'

'We will proceed back to Shagfe with all speed. First, pour out a cup of water. This creature was pent for several days.'

Fabrache poured with a rueful smirk, as if reflecting upon the odd quirks of fate to which he was continually subjected. The creature without hesitation turned the contents of the cup into its throat, and did the same for three more cupfuls. Ifness then proffered a cake of jellied meat, which the creature cautiously refused, then dried fruit, which it dropped into its throat. Ifness offered it pounded seeds from which Fabrache made his bread, salt, and lump-fat, all of which the creature rejected.

The supplies were redistributed, and the dark creature was mounted on the pack animal, which jerked and shuddered at the alien scent, and walked with stiff legs and rounded nostrils.

The four set off down the Vurush Valley, along the route they had come, and the miles fell back into the afternoon. The alien rode stolidly, showing no interest in the landscape, hardly moving in the saddle. Etzwane asked Ifness, 'Do you think it is in a state of shock, or grief or terror? Or is it only semi-intelligent?'

'As yet, we have no basis for assessment. In due course I would hope to learn a great deal.'

'Perhaps it could act as interpreter between men and asutra,' said Etzwane.

Ifness frowned, a signal that the idea had not yet occurred to him. 'This is of course a possibility.' He looked towards Fabrache, who had drawn up his pacer. 'What is the matter?'

Fabrache pointed to the east, where the slopes of the Orgai eased down upon the plain. 'A party of riders – six or eight.'

Ifness rose in his saddle, gazed across the distance. 'They are riding in our direction at a good rate of speed.'

'We had best do likewise,' said Fabrache. 'In this land one cannot take the friendship of strangers for granted.' He jerked his pacer into a full lope and the others followed suit, Etzwane applying the quirt to the pacer ridden by the alien.

Down the valley they coursed, Ifness frowning in distaste. The alien rode stiffly erect, clutching the back-curving horns of his beast. Etzwane judged that for the first two miles they gained ground, then for another two miles held their own, then the pursuing band seemed to gain. Fabrache, with long frame crouched grotesquely low and beard flapping over his shoulder, urged his pacer to its utmost efforts. He yelled over his shoulder, 'It is Hozman Sore-throat and his slaving band! Ride for freedom! Ride for your life!'

The pacers were tiring. Time after time they stumbled into a lurching jog, which aroused Fabrache to frantic measures. The pursuing pacers had also become winded, and they too slackened speed. The suns were low in the west, laying three trails upon the surface of the Vurush, Fabrache appraised the distance to the pursuing band and measured it against the height of the suns. He gave a call of despair. 'We will be slaves before dark, and then we will learn Hozman's secret.'

Ifness pointed ahead. 'There, on the shore, a camp of wagons.'

Fabrache peered and gave a croak of hope. 'We shall arrive in time and claim protection . . . Unless they are cannibals, we are in luck.'

A few moments later he called back, 'They are the Alula; I now recognise their wains. They are a hospitable folk and we are safe.'

On a level area near the river, fifty wains with crooked eight-foot wheels had been drawn up to form a hollow square, the wheels and dropped sideboards creating a staunch fence. A single opening faced the river. The slavers, trailing by three hundred yards, their pacers coughing and stumbling, gave up the chase and swerved aside towards the river.

Fabrache led the way around the wall of wains and halted before the opening. Four men jumped forward in a crouching, splay-legged posture of threat. They wore jerkins of black chumpa-hide strips, helmets of black leather, and carried crossbows three feet wide. 'If you be riders with the group yonder, go your way. We want no business with you.'

Fabrache leapt from his pacer and stepped forward. 'Put aside your weapons! We are travelers of the Orgai and fugitives from Hozman Sore-throat! We request protection for the night.'

'All very well, but what of that one-eyed demoniac creature? We have heard tales; it is a Red Devil!'

'Nothing of the sort! The Red Devils are all dead,

killed in a recent battle. This is the sole survivor of a wrecked spaceship.'

'In that case, kill it as well. Why should we nurture off-world enemies?'

Ifness spoke in a measured and aristocratic voice, 'The matter is more complicated than this. I intend to learn the language of this creature, if it is able to talk. This knowledge will help us defeat our enemies.'

'It is a matter for Karazan. Stand in your tracks; we are a suspicious people.'

A moment later an enormous man strode forward, taller by a head than Fabrache. His face was no less impressive than his bulk; keen eyes glittered under a broad brow, a short beard clothed his cheeks and chin. He required a single second to appraise the situation, then turned a glance of contemptuous derogation towards the guards. 'What is the difficulty? When have Alula feared three men and a monster? Let them in.' He scowled down at the riverbank where Hozman Sore-throat and his band rested their pacers, then sauntered back the way he had come. The warriors put aside their crossbows and stood back. 'Enter as you will. Take your pacers to the pen. Bed yourselves where you like, except in company with our wives.'

'You have our gratitude,' Fabrache declared. 'Mind, that is Hozman Sore-throat, the expert slaver, yonder; let no one stray outside the camp, or he will never to be seen again.'

Etzwane was intrigued by the camp, and by certain elements of barbaric splendor which in the popular imagination of Shant characterised all the tribes of Caraz. The green, pink, and magenta tents had been embroidered in marvelous starbursts and radiants. The carved tent stakes stood eight feet tall, displaying fetishes of four sorts: winged scorpions, wisk-weasels, Lake Nior kingfish, Lake Nior pelicans. The men of the camp wore trousers of pounded ahulph leather, glossy black boots, embroidered vests over loose white blouses. Married women wound their heads with purple and green scarves, their full gowns were of various colors; girls, however, swaggered about in breeches and boots like the men. Before each tent a cauldron bubbled over a fire, and the odors of spices and stewing meat permeated the camp. In front of the ceremonial wain sat the elders, passing a leather flask of aquavita back and forth. Near by four other men, each wearing a string of golden beads, made desultory music upon stringed instruments.

No one gave the newcomers more than cursory attention; they went to the area indicated to them, unloaded their pacers, and laid out their beds. The alien watched without apparent interest. Fabrache dared not go to the river for clams or crayfish and cooked an austere meal of porridge and dried meat; the alien drank water and thrust a quantity of porridge into its maw without enthusiasm. Children of the camp began to gather and watched in wide-eyed wonder. They were joined by others, progressively older, and presently one put a timid question, 'Is the creature tame?'

'It seems to be,' said Etzwane. 'It came to Durdane in a spaceship, so it is certainly civilised.'

'Is it your slave?' asked another.

'Not exactly. We rescued it from a wrecked spaceship, and now we want to learn how to talk to it.'

'Can it do wonderful magic?'

'Not to my knowledge.'

'Does it dance?' asked one of the girls. 'Bring it to where the music is played and we will watch its fanciful acts.'

'It neither dances nor plays music,' said Etzwane.

'What a tiresome beast.'

A woman came to scold the children and sent them about their business, and the group was left in peace.

Fabrache spoke to Ifness. 'How do you intend to keep the creature for the night? Must we stand a guard?'

'I think not,' said Ifness. 'It might then consider itself a prisoner and seek to escape. It knows that we are its source of food and security, and I believe that it will stay with us of its own volition. Still we will maintain an unobtrusive watch.' Ifness now addressed himself to the creature and attempted the rudiments of communication: placing down first one pebble, then two, then three, while saying 'One . . . two . . . three . . . ' and signaling the alien to do likewise, but to no avail. Ifness next directed the creature's attention to the sky, where the stars blazed bright and clear. Ifness pointed here and there in a questioning fashion, and even took the creature's hard finger and pointed it about the sky. 'It is either extremely intelligent or extremely stupid,' grumbled Ifness. 'Still, were the asutra in command we would derive no more information. There is no cause for complaint.'

From the central fire came the sound of energetic music, and Etzwane went to watch the dancing. The youths and maidens, forming into lines, swayed, kicked, capered, swung each other in circles, all in the most exuberant fashion. The music seemed uncomplicated to Etzwane, even somewhat naive, but as vigorous and forthright as the dancing. Some of the girls were extremely handsome, he thought, and showed little diffidence . . . He toyed with the idea of playing music and went so far as to examine a spare instrument of bizarre and exaggerated construction. He sounded the strings, but the frets were oddly spaced and tuning was to a strange mode. Etzwane doubted his ability to use the instrument. He struck a few chords, using his usual fingering. The results were strange but not displeasing. A girl stood over him, smiling. 'Do you play music?'

'Yes, but this instrument is unfamiliar to me.'

'What is your race and fetish?'

'I am a man of Shant; I was born a Chilite in Canton Bastern.'

The girl shook her head in bewilderment. 'They must be far lands; I have never heard of them. Are you a slave-taker?'

'No. My friend and I came to look at the strange space-ships.'

'Such things are interesting.'

The girl was pretty, vivacious, and beautifully formed, and Etzwane thought that she seemed pleasantly disposed. He suddenly felt an inclination to play music, and bent his head over the instrument to learn its system of harmonics . . . He returned the strings, and found that by thinking in the unusual Kudarian mode the instrument fell under his control. He cautiously played a few phrases, and tried to follow the music, with a degree of success.

'Come,' said the girl. She took him to the other musicians and brought him the leather flask from which all had been drinking. Etzwane allowed himself a cautious swallow; the sting of the spirit caused him to laugh and blow out his breath. 'Laugh again!' the girl commanded. 'Musicians should never be somber, even when their mood is tragic; their eyes should show colored lights.'

One of the musicians glowered first at the girl then at Etzwane, who decided to be discreet. He played tentative chords, and with increasing confidence joined the music. The theme was simple and played insistently again and again, but each time with a small alteration: the prolongation of a beat, a twanged note, a trifle of emphasis here or there. The musicians seemed to vie in producing the most subtle changes in the succession; and meanwhile the music became even more intense and compelling, and the dancers swirled, jerked arms, kicked, and stamped in the firelight . . . Etzwane began to wonder when the music would stop, and how. The others would know the signal; they would try to catch him napping, so that when he played on alone he would seem ridiculous: an ancient prank to work upon the stranger. All would know when the tune should end; there would be a side-glance, a raised elbow, a hiss, a shift of position . . . The signal came; Etzwane felt its presence. As he had expected, the music stopped short; he instantly broke into a variation in a different mode, a pulsing statement even more compelling than the first theme, and presently the musicians, some grinning, some with wry winces, again joined the music . . . Etzwane laughed and bent over the instrument, which now had become familiar, and began to produce runs and trills . . . The music at last halted. The girl came to sit beside Etzwane and proffered the flask of spirit. Etzwane drank and, putting down the flask, asked, 'What is your name?'

'I am Rune the Willow Wand, of the Pelican fetish. Who are you?'

'My name is Gastel Etzwane. In Shant we do not reckon our clans or fetishes, only our canton. And, as it used to be, the colors of our torc, which now we wear no more.'

'In different lands are different customs,' agreed the girl. 'Sometimes it is puzzling. Over the Orgai and along the Botgarsk River live the Shada, who cut off a girl's ears if she so much as speaks to a man. Is this the custom of Shant?'

'Not at all,' said Etzwane. 'Among the Alula are you allowed to speak to strangers?'

'Yes, indeed; we obey our own inclinations in such matters; and why should we not?' She tilted her head and gave Etzwane a candid inspection. 'You are of a race thinner and keener than ours. You have what we call the *aersk** look.'

Etzwane was not displeased by the flattery. The girl apparently was somewhat wayward and wanted to enlarge her horizons by flirting with a strange young man. Etzwane, though of a wary disposition, was not unwilling to oblige her. He asked, 'The musician yonder: he is not your betrothed?'

'Galgar the Wisk-weasel? Do I seem the sort who would consort with a man like Galgar?'

'Of course not. I notice also that he keeps poor time in his music, which indicates a deficient personality.'

'You are amazingly perceptive,' said Rune the Willow Wand. She moved closer; Etzwane smelled the tree-balsam she used as a scent. She spoke in a soft voice, 'Do you like my cap?'

'Yes, of course,' said Etzwane, puzzled by the lack of sequence in the girl's remarks. 'Although it seems about to fall off your head.'

Ifness had come to sit by the fire. He now raised an admonitory finger, and Etzwane went to learn his requirements. 'A word of caution,' said Ifness.

'Unnecessary. I am more than cautious; I look in all directions at once.'

'Just so, just so. Remember that in the Alul camp we are subject to their laws. Fabrache tells me that the Alul women can assert a marital connection with some simplicity. Do you notice how certain of the maidens wear their caps askew? If a man removes the cap or so much as sets it straight, he is held to have disarranged her intimate apparel, and if she raises an outcry, the two must marry.'

Etzwane looked through the dying firelight towards

* *Aersk:* untranslatable. Loosely, a fearless nobleman of the high crags, whose first needs are space, sunlight, and storms.

Rune the Willow Wand. 'The caps are precariously placed . . . An interesting custom.' He slowly went to rejoin the girl. She asked, 'What has that peculiar person been telling you?'

Etzwane cast about for a reply. 'He noticed my interest in you; he warned me not to compromise myself or offend you by touching your garments.'

Rune the Willow Wand smiled and cast a contemptuous glance towards Ifness. 'What an old prig! But he need not fear! My three best friends have arranged to meet their lovers near the river and I agreed to walk with them, although I have no lover and will be wistful and lonely.'

'I advise you to walk some other night,' said Etzwane. 'Hozman Sore-throat prowls the vicinity; he is the arch-slaver of Caraz.'

'Pff. Do you refer to the rogues who chased you hither? They rode north; they are gone. They would never dare molest the Alula.'

Etzwane gave his head a skeptical shake. 'If you are lonely, come talk to me yonder behind the wain where I have spread my blankets.'

Rune the Willow Wand stood back, eyebrows arched in disdain. 'I am not interested in such a graceless proceeding. To think that I considered you *aersk*.' She twitched her cap securely down on her head and sauntered away. Etzwane gave a rueful shrug and presently went to his blankets. For a period he watched the alien, who sat motionless in the shadows, showing only its outline and the soft glow of its single eye.

Etzwane felt somewhat reluctant to sleep with the alien so near at hand; after all, they knew nothing of its proclivities. But presently he drowsed . . . After a time he awoke uneasily, but the creature sat immobile, and Etzwane went back to sleep once more.

An hour before dawn a bellow of enormous rage jerked Etzwane from his slumber. He jumped to his feet to see a number of Alul warriors rushing forth from their wains. They spoke back and forth, then all dashed for their pacers, and presently Etzwane heard the thud of retreating hooves.

Fabrache had gone forth for information; he returned, dolefully wagging his head. 'It's just as I warned them and they would not believe. Last night four maidens went to walk down by the river and never returned. Hozman Sore-throat is to blame. The Alula ride in vain, for once Hozman makes his pluck his victims are never seen again.'

The riders returned disconsolate; they had cast about for tracks without success, and they had no ahulphs to follow the slave-taker's trail. The leader of the search party was the massive Karazan. He flung himself from the saddle and marched across the compound to confront Ifness. 'Tell me where the slave-taker may be found, that we may either win back our flesh and blood or pull him apart with our bare hands.'

Ifness indicated Fabrache. 'My friend here, also a slaver, can provide information far more detailed and intimate than I.'

Fabrache gave his beard a judicious tug. 'I know nothing of Hozman Sore-throat, neither his race, nor his clan, nor his fetish. I can assure you of two facts only. First, he often visits Shagfe, to buy at the collecting station; and second, whoever Hozman takes is gone forever.'

'That remains to be seen,' said Karazan. 'Where is Shagfe?'

'A day's journey to the east.'

'We ride at once for Shagfe! Bring forth the pacers!'

'Our own destination is Shagfe,' said Ifness. 'We will ride in your company.'

'Make haste,' said the Alula. 'Our mission will not be conducive to leisure or reverie.'

Eighteen pacers loped across the Wild Waste, the riders slouched low, capes flapping over their shoulders. Shagfe appeared in the distance: a gray and black smudge upon the violet-gray background of hills and haze.

At sunset the riders pounded into Shagfe, to halt in a swirl of dust before the inn.

Baba looked through the door-hole, pale eyebrows in astounded arcs at the sight of the alien creature. The Alula descended and entered, with Ifness, Fabrache, Etzwane, and the silent black creature coming behind.

At the benches hunched the Kash Blue-worms, drunk and surly. At the sight of their tribal enemies, the Alula, they drew themselves up and muttered together. Fabrache spoke to Baba, 'My friends here have a bit of business with Hozman Sore-throat. Has he been seen today?'

Baba said peevishly, 'I make a rule against discussing the affairs of my customers. I am not – '

Karazan strode forward, to loom above Baba. 'Answer the question.'

'I have not seen Hozman since early this morning,' growled Baba.

'Aha, what's this? Early morning?'

'True! With these two hands I served his gruel while the suns clambered over the horizon.'

'How can this be?' Karazan demanded in a menacing voice. 'He was seen at sundown where the Vurush comes down from the Orgai. At midnight he made his presence felt. How could he have eaten breakfast here at dawn?'

The innkeeper reflected. 'It might be possible, on a good Angos pacer.'

'Well then, what was his pacer this morning?'

'An ordinary Jerzy.'

'Perhaps he changed his mount,' Ifness suggested.

The Alula snorted. He turned back to Fabrache. 'You can certify that Hozman chased you down the Orgai Mountains?'

'I am sure. Have I not seen Hozman Sore-throat many a time, riding with his band and alone?'

A voice spoke to their backs. 'I hear my name mentioned, I trust in a kindly reference.'

All swung about. Hozman Sore-throat stood in the door-hole. He came forward, a pale, stern-faced man of ordinary stature. A black cloak concealed his garments, except for the maroon scarf which muffled his neck.

The Alula said, 'Last night on the river Vurush you took four of our people. We want them restored to us. The Alula are not for the slave pens; this we will make clear to every slave-taker of Caraz.'

Hozman Sore-throat laughed, putting aside the threat with the ease of long practice. 'Are you not over hasty? You accost me without basis.'

Karazan took a slow step forward. 'Hozman, your time is upon you.'

The landlord bustled close. 'Not in the inn! This is the first law of Shagfe!'

The Alula thrust him aside with a sweep of his massive arm. 'Where are our people?'

'Come now,' said Hozman briskly. 'I can't be blamed for every disappearance in the Mirkil district. At Vurush River under the Orgais? Last night? A far distance for a man who breakfasted at Shagfe.'

'A not impossible distance.'

Hozman smilingly shook his head. 'If I owned pacers that staunch and swift, would I deal in slaves? I would breed pacers and make my fortune. As for your people, the Orgai is chumpa country; here may be the tragic truth.'

Karazan, pale with rage and frustration, stood speechless, unable to find a crevice in Hozman's defense. Hozman glimpsed the black creature in the shadow of the doorway. He jerked forward, intent and startled. 'What does the Ka do here? Is it now your ally?'

Ifness said evenly, 'I captured it under Thrie Orgai, near where you met us yesterday afternoon.'

Hozman turned away from the creature he had called a 'Ka'; nevertheless his eyes strayed back towards where it stood. He spoke in easy, jocular tones, 'Another voice, another accusation! If words were blades, poor Hozman would writhe on the ground in a hundred pieces.'

'As he will, in any event,' said Karazan menacingly, 'unless he returns the four Alul girls he stole.'

Hozman calculated, looking back and forth between Ifness and the Ka. He turned to Karazan. 'Certain of the chumpas are my agents,' he said in a voice like cream. 'Perhaps they hold your Alul girls. If such is the case, will you trade four for two?'

'How do you mean, "four for two"?' growled Karazan.

'For your four, I'll take this white-haired man and the Ka.'

'I veto the proposal,' said Ifness promptly. 'You must put forward a better offer.'

'Well, the Ka alone then. Think! A savage alien for four handsome girls.'

'A remarkable offer!' declared Ifness. 'Why do you want the creature?'

'I can always find customers for such a curiosity.' Hozman moved politely aside to allow newcomers into the common room: two Kash Blue-worms, drunk and ugly, the hair matted on their foreheads. The foremost jostled Hozman. 'Stand back, reptile. You have brought us all to poverty and degradation; must you now block my path as well?'

Hozman moved away, his lips curling in a smile of contempt. The Kash Blue-worm stopped short and thrust forward his face. 'Do you dare to mock me? Am I ludicrous?'

Baba sprang forward. 'No combat in here, never in the common room!'

The Kash swung his arm in a backhanded blow, knocking Hozman to the floor, at which Baba brought forth a cudgel and with amazing dexterity drove the Kash cursing and lumbering from the inn. Ifness solicitously reached to help Hozman to his feet. He glanced at Etzwane. 'Your knife, to cut off a growth.'

Etzwane jumped forward. Ifness held aside Hozman's maroon scarf; Etzwane slashed the straps of the little harness, while Hozman lay thrashing and kicking. The innkeeper gaped in amazement, unable to wield his cudgel. With his nose wrinkled in distaste Ifness lifted the asutra, a flattened creature marked with faint brown and maroon stripes. Etzwane slashed the nerve and Hozman emitted the most appalling scream yet heard in the inn at Shagfe.

A hard, strong shape struck between Ifness and Etzwane: the Ka. Etzwane raised his knife, ready to stab, but the Ka was already gone with the asutra and out into the yard. Ifness ran in pursuit, with Etzwane close behind. They came upon a macabre scene, indistinct in swirls of boiling dust. The Ka, talons protruding from its feet, stamped upon the asutra and tore it to shreds.

Ifness, putting away his energy gun, stood grimly watching. Etzwane said in astonishment, 'It hates the asutra more than we do.'

'A curious exhibition,' Ifness agreed.

From within the inn came a new outcry and the thud of blows. Clutching his head, Hozman ran frantically out into the yard, with the Alula in pursuit. Ifness, moving with unusual haste, intervened and waved off the Alula.

'Are you totally without foresight? If you kill this man we will learn nothing.'

'What is there to learn?' roared Karazan. 'He has sold our daughters into slavery; he says we will never see them again.'

'Why not learn the details?' Ifness turned to where Etzwane prevented Hozman from flight. 'You have much to tell us.'

'What can I tell you?' said Hozman. 'Why should I trouble myself? They will tear me apart like the cannibals they are.'

'I am nevertheless curious. You may tell your story.'

'It is a dream,' mumbled Hozman. 'I rode through the air like a gray ghost, I spoke with monsters; I am a creature alive and dead.'

'First of all,' said Ifness, 'where are the people you stole last night?'

Hozman threw his arm up in an unrestrained gesture which suggested imprecision in his thinking processes. 'Beyond the sky! They are gone forever. No one returns after the car drops down.'

'Ah, I see. They have been taken into an aircraft.'

'Better to say that they are gone from the world Durdane.'

'And when does the car drop down?'

Hozman looked furtively aside, with his mouth pinched into a crafty knot. Ifness spoke sharply, 'No temporising! The Alula are waiting to torture you and we must not inconvenience them.'

Hozman gave a hoarse laugh. 'What do I care for torture? I know I must die by pain; so I was told by my witch-uncle. Kill me any way you like; I have no preference.'

'How long have you carried the asutra?'

'It has been so long I have forgotten my old life . . .

When? Ten years ago, twenty years. They looked into my tent, two men in black garments; they were no men of Caraz, nor men of Durdane. I rose to meet them in fear, and they put the mentor upon me.' Hozman felt his neck with trembling fingers. He looked sidelong towards the Alula, who stood attentive, hands at the hilts of their scimitars.

'Where are the four you stole from us?' asked Karazan.

'They are gone to a far world. You are curious as to what is to be their lot? I cannot say. The mentor told me nothing.'

Ifness made a sign to Karazan and spoke in an easy voice, 'The mentor was able to communicate with you?'

Hozman's eyes became unfocused, words began to gush from his mouth. 'It is a condition impossible to describe. When I first discovered the creature I went crazy with revulsion – but only for a moment! It performed what I call a pleasure-trick, and I became flooded with joy. The dreary Balch swamp seemed to swim with delightful odors, and I was a man transformed. There was at that moment nothing which I could not have accomplished!' Hozman threw his arms to the sky. 'The mood lasted several minutes, and then the men in black returned and made me aware of my duties. I obeyed, for I quickly learned the penalty of disobedience; the mentor could bless with joy or punish with pain. It knew the language of men but could not speak except in a hiss and a whistle, which I never learned. But I could talk aloud and ask if such a course fulfilled its wishes. The mentor became my soul, closer to me than hands and feet, for its nerves led to my nerves. It was alert to my welfare and never forced me to work in rain or cold. And I never hungered, for my work was rewarded with ingots of good gold and copper and sometimes steel.'

'And what were your duties?' asked Ifness.

Hozman's flow of words was again stimulated, as if they had long been pent inside of him, building a pressure to be released. 'They were simple. I bought prime slaves, as many as could be had. I worked as a slave-taker, and I have scoured the face of Caraz, from the Azur River in the east to the vast Duglov in the west, and as far south as Mount Thruska. Thousands of slaves have I sent into space!'

'How did you so send them?'

'At night, when no one was near and the mentor could warn me of danger, I called down the little car and loaded aboard my slaves, which first I had drugged into a happy stupor: sometimes only one or two, again as many as a dozen or even more. If I chose, the car would take me where I wished to go, quickly through the night, as from the Orgai to Shagfe village.'

'And where did the car take the slaves?'

Hozman pointed into the sky. 'Above hangs a depot hull, where the slaves lie quiet. When the hull is full it flies away to the mentor's world, which lies somewhere in the coils of Histhorbo the Snake. So much I learned to my idle amusement one starry night when I asked my mentor many questions, which it answered by a yes or a no. Why did it need so many slaves? Because its previous creatures were inadequate and insubordinate, and because it feared a terrible enemy, somewhere off among the stars.' Hozman fell silent. The Alula had drawn close to surround him; they now regarded him less with hate than with awe for the weird travail he had undergone.

Ifness asked in his most casual voice, 'And how do you call down the little car?'

Hozman licked his lips and looked off over the plain. Ifness said gently, 'Never again will you carry the asutra which brought such bliss to your brain. You are now one with the rest of us, and we consider the asutra our enemies.'

Hozman said sullenly, 'In my pouch I carry a box with a little button within. When I require the car, I go out into the dark night and push on the button and hold it so until the car comes down.'

'Who drives the car?'

'The device works by a mysterious will of its own.'

'Give me the box with the button.'

Hozman slowly drew forth the box, which Ifness took into his own possession. Etzwane, at a glance and a nod from Ifness, searched Hozman's pouch and person, but found only three small ingots of copper and a magnificent steel dagger with a handle of carved white glass.

Hozman watched with a quizzical expression. 'Now what will you do with me?'

Ifness looked towards Karazan, who shook his head. 'This is not a man upon whom we can take vengeance. He is a puppet, a toy on a string.'

'You have made a just decision,' said Ifness. 'In this slave-taking land his offense is simple overzealousness.'

'Still, what next?' demanded Karazan, 'We have not reclaimed our daughters. This man must call down the car, which we will seize and hold against their release.'

'There is no one aboard the car with whom you can bargain,' said Hozman. Suddenly he added, 'You might go aloft in the car and expostulate in person.'

Karazan uttered a soft sound and looked up into the purple sky of the evening: a colossus in white blouse and black breeches. Etzwane also looked up and thought of Rune the Willow Wand among the crawling asutra . . .

Ifness asked Hozman, 'Have you ever gone aloft to the depot ship?'

'Not I,' said Hozman. 'I had great fear of such an event. On occasion a gray dwarf creature and its mentor came down to the planet. Often have I stood hours through the night while the two mentors hissed one to the other. Then I knew that the depot had reached capacity and that no more slaves were needed for a period.'

'When last did the mentor come down from the depot?'

'A time ago; I cannot recall exactly. I have been allowed small time for reflection.'

Ifness became pensive. Karazan thrust his bulk forward. 'This shall be our course of action: we shall call down the car and ourselves go aloft, to destroy our enemies and liberate our people. We need only wait until night.'

'The tactic leaps to mind,' said Ifness. 'If successful it might yield valuable benefits – not the least being the ship itself. But difficulties present themselves, notably the return descent. You might find yourself in command of the depot ship, but none the less marooned. Such a venture is precarious. I advise against it.'

Karazan made a disconsolate sound and again searched the sky, as if to discover a feasible route to the depot ship. Hozman, seeing an opportunity to slip away unobserved, did so. He walked around the inn to his pacer, to find a Blue-worm rifling the saddlebags. Hozman gave an inarticulate babble of fury and leapt upon the burly back. A second Blue-worm, at the other side of the pacer, drove his fist into Hozman's face, to send Hozman staggering back against the wall of the inn. The Blue-worms continued their ignoble work. The Alula looked on with disgust, half of a mind to intervene, but Karazan called them away. 'Let the jackals do as they will; it is none of our affair.'

'You call us jackals?' demanded one of the Kash. 'That is an insulting epithet!'

'Only for a creature who is not a jackal,' said Karazan in a bored voice. 'You need not take offense.'

The Kash, considerably outnumbered, had no real stomach for a fight and turned back to the saddlebags. Karazan turned away and shook his fist at the sky.

Etzwane, restless and troubled, spoke to Ifness. 'Suppose for a fact that we did capture the ship. Could you not bring it down to the ground?'

'Almost certainly I could not. With definite certainty I do not intend to try.'

Etzwane stared at Ifness with cold hostility. 'We must do something. A hundred, perhaps two hundred people hang up there, waiting for the asutra to take them away to some strange place, and we are the only ones who can help them.'

Ifness laughed. 'You exaggerate my capabilities, at least. I suspect that you have been captivated by certain flirtatious glances and that now you wish to perform a gallant feat, no matter what the difficulties.'

Etzwane contained his first rush of words, especially since the remarks were apt enough to cause him discomfort . . . Why should he suddenly expect altruism from Ifness, after all? From the moment of their first meeting Ifness had consistently refused to divert himself from his own large concerns. Not for the first time, Etzwane regarded Ifness with cold dislike. Their relationship, never close, had shifted into a new and distant phase. But he spoke in an even voice, 'At Shillinsk, could you not call Dasconetta and request an Earth ship for a business of great urgency?'

'I could do this,' said Ifness. 'Furthermore, Dasconetta might well put through the order, and thereby sequester to himself an achievement which rightfully should be credited elsewhere.'

'How long before such a ship could arrive at Shagfe?'

'As to this, I could make no estimate.'

'Within a day? Three days? Two weeks? A month?'

'A number of factors are involved. Under favorable conditions a ship might arrive in two weeks.'

Karazan, comprehending nothing of the matter save the time-span involved, declared, 'By that time the depot may be gone, and the people as well, to terrible events on some far, cold world.'

'It is a tragic situation,' agreed Ifness, 'but I can make no recommendations.'

'What of this?' asked Etzwane. 'You ride at best speed to Shillinsk, and there demand assistance from Dasconetta. I will call down the transfer car and go up with the Alula to capture the depot ship. If possible we will return to Durdane; if not we will await your coming.'

Ifness reflected a moment before replying. 'The scheme has a certain mad logic, and conceivably might come to a successful issue. I know a tactic to obviate Dasconetta's interference, which goes to answer one of my previous objections . . . The uncertainties however are numerous; you are dealing with an unknown situation.'

'I understand this,' said Etzwane. 'But the Alula will go aloft in any event and here' – he patted his pouch with the energy gun within – 'is their best hope of success. Knowing this, how could I stand aside?'

Ifness shrugged. 'I personally cannot afford these quixotic extravagances; I would long since have been dead. Still, if you bring down to Durdane an alien spaceship, or even secure it in orbit until my coming, I shall applaud your altruistic bravado. I emphasise, however, that while I will keep your affairs in mind, I can guarantee nothing, and I strongly recommend that you stay below.'

Etzwane gave a bitter chuckle. 'I understand very well. Still, human lives are at stake whether we go up or not. You had best leave for Shillinsk at once. Haste is essential.'

Ifness frowned. 'Tonight? The way is long . . . Still, Baba's inn offers only small solace. I agree; haste is desirable. Well then, the Ka and I will ride for Shillinsk with Fabrache to guide us. We leave at once.'

Chapter 7

The suns were three hours gone beyond the far Orgai, and the last purple glow had left the sky. On the plain waited eighteen Alul warriors, with Etzwane and Hozman.

'Here is my usual spot,' said Hozman, 'and now is my ordinary time. The routine is this. I press the button. After twenty minutes I look for a green light overhead. I then release the button and the car lands. My slaves stand in an orderly line. They are drugged and obedient, but not aware, like people in a dream. The door opens and a pale-blue light issues forth. I move forward, marshaling the slaves. If the car contains a mentor it appears on the ledge, and then I must wait while the mentors converse. When the slaves are within and the conversation at an end, I close the door and the car departs. There is no more to be told.'

'Very good. Press the button.'

Hozman did as instructed. 'How often have I done this deed,' he murmured. 'Always I wondered where they went and how they passed their lives. Then, after the car departed, I would look up into the sky and consider the stars . . . But no more, no more. I shall take your pacers to Shagfe and sell them to Baba, and then I shall return to the land where I was born and become a professional seer

. . . Stand in line, close together. You must seem vague and limp.'

The group formed a line and waited. The night was silent. Five miles to the north lay Shagfe, but the fires and oil lamps flickered too dimly to be seen. The minutes passed slowly; Etzwane had never known time so to prolong itself. Each second stretched elastically and departed with reluctance into the past.

Hozman held up his hand. 'The green light . . . The car comes down. I now release the button. Stand ready – but limp and easy; make no moves . . .'

Above sounded a faint sigh and a hum; a dark shape moved across the stars and settled fifty or sixty yards away. An aperture slowly appeared, casting a wan blue glow upon the ground. 'Come,' muttered Hozman. 'In a line, close together . . . There crawls the mentor. You must be quick – but not hasty.'

Etzwane halted at the entrance. A blue glow showed the way within. On a ledge beside a row of colored lights rested an asutra. For an instant Etzwane and asutra looked eye to eye; then the asutra, apprehending its danger, hissed and scuttled backward towards a small passage. Etzwane swung his blade, to chop away the creature's abdomen and block its escape. In revulsion he scraped the jerking parts to the deck, where they were crushed under Alul boots.

Hozman gave a whinny of crazy, high-pitched laughter. 'I am not yet free of the thing's influence; I could feel its emotion. It was furiously angry.'

Karazan pushed into the interior, and the ceiling pressed down upon his head. 'Come, let us do the business while our blood flows hot! Gastel Etzwane, do you understand the use of these swivels and pegs and blinking ghost-lamps?'

'I do not.'

'Come in then; we go to do what we must.'

Etzwane was last to enter. He hesitated, beset by the certain knowledge that their plans were insanely rash. 'On this consideration alone may we expect success,' he told himself hollowly. He looked back into Hozman's face and surprised an expression curiously vital and eager, as if Hozman could hardly keep from shouting aloud in joy.

Here is his revenge, Etzwane gloomily told himself: on us and on the asutra as well. He will go forth now to take vengeance on all Durdane for the horror which has been his life . . . Best that I should kill him now . . . Etzwane paused in the doorway. Outside, Hozman stood expectantly; within, the Alula, incipiently claustrophobic, began to grumble. On a sudden impulse Etzwane jumped back to the ground and jerked at Hozman's arm, which was crooked somewhat behind his back. In his hand he carried a length of white rag Etzwane looked slowly up into Hozman's face. Hozman licked his lips, his brows dropping hangdog low at the outer corners.

'So, then,' said Etzwane, 'you would signal us to our doom, with all the others on the ship.'

'No, no,' stammered Hozman. 'This is my kerchief. It is a habit, no more; I wipe my sweating palms.'

'They sweat understandably,' said Etzwane.

Karazan lurched forth from the car. He apprehended the situation in an instant and turned a terrible stare upon Hozman. 'For this act you can blame no mentor, no evil force which compelled you.' He drew his great scimitar. 'Hozman, on your knees and bend your neck, for your time has come.'

'A moment,' said Etzwane. 'What is the system to closing the door?'

'You must puzzle it out for yourself,' said Hozman. He attempted to spring away, but Karazan lunged to catch the collar of his cape.

Hozman began to plead in a hysterical, tearful voice. 'This is not according to our arrangement! And also, I can supply information to save your lives, but unless you guarantee my freedom, you will never hear it; you may kill me first, and then, while you slave on a far distant world, remember this laugh of mine.' He threw back his head and uttered a wild wail of mockery. 'And you will know I died happy, for I brought ruin to my enemies!'

Etzwane said, 'We don't want your miserable life; we hope to save our own, and your treachery is our worst danger.'

'There will be no more treachery! I trade my life and freedom for your own!'

'Thrust him inside,' said Etzwane. 'If we live, he lives, and upon our return he shall have a flogging.'

'No, no, no!' screamed Hozman. Karazan cuffed him to silence.

'I would prefer to kill the vermin,' said Karazan. 'In with you.' He thrust Hozman into the car. Etzwane studied the door and discovered the inside clamp. He asked Hozman, 'What now? Do I pull the door closed and throw this lever?'

'That is all,' came Hozman's sullen reply. 'The car will leave Durdane of its own volition.'

'Then make ready; we are about to leave.'

Etzwane closed the door. At once the floor thrust into their feet. The Alula gasped, Hozman whimpered. There was a period of acceleration, then ease. The blue illumination made faces unrecognisable and seemed to educe a new dimension of each man's soul. Etzwane, looking on the Alula, felt humble in the face of their bravery; unlike himself, they knew nothing of Ifness' abilities. Then Etzwane asked of Hozman: 'What is this knowledge by which you will save our lives?'

'It is nothing definite,' said Hozman. 'It concerns your

general demeanor and how you must act to avoid instant detection.'

'Well, then, how must we act?'

'You must walk like this, with your arms limp, your eyes blank and mild, your legs loose, as if they barely supported the weight of your bodies.' Hozman stood limp and futile, with long, hopeless creases pinching his face.

Fifteen minutes the speed held, then slackened. Hozman said nervously, 'I know nothing of conditions aboard – but you must strike hard and fast, and make the most of surprise.'

'The asutra ride their hosts?'

'I imagine that they do.'

'For your own sake,' said Etzwane, 'fight and fight well.'

Hozman made no response. A moment passed. The car touched a solid object and slid into a socket, with a small shock of finality. The men tensed themselves. The door opened. They looked into an empty corridor, along which men might walk single file. A voice came from a panel: 'Step forth into the hall; remove all clothing; you will be cleansed by a refreshing spray.'

'Act as if you are too drugged to understand the instruction,' muttered Hozman.

Etzwane moved slowly out into the corridor and languidly walked to the far end, where a door barred the way. The Alula followed, Hozman shambling in their midst. The voice spoke again, 'Remove all clothes; they must be removed.'

Etzwane made tentative motions to obey, then let his arms sag, as if fatigued, and sagged against the wall. From the speaker came a faint hiss and a disgusted mutter. From ceiling orifices jets of an acrid liquid struck down, drenching them to the skin . . . The jets were cut off; the end door opened. Etzwane staggered through into a large circular chamber. Here waited half a dozen biped creatures, gray and lumpy of skin, squat in stature, batrachian in aspect. Five eyes like orbs of milk-glass protruded from the squat heads; the feet were flaps of gray-green muscle. On the nape of each neck rested an asutra. Etzwane had no need to call a signal. Pent energy exploded within the Alula; they lurched forward; in five seconds the gray host-things lay dead in spouts of gray-green blood, with the asutra crushed and hacked. Etzwane glared around the room, nostrils dilated, the energy gun in readiness. But no new gray creatures appeared. He ran on long, stealthy steps to the end of the chamber, where narrow corridors led in two directions. He listened and heard no sound save a low pulsing hum. Half the Alula set off with Karazan to the left; Etzwane led the others to the right. The corridors, narrow and low, had been built to asutra concepts of scale; Etzwane wondered how Karazan fared. He came to a narrow ramp; at the top he saw the gleam of stars. Up he clambered at his best speed and burst out into a control dome. A low bench circled the room; at one area a dozen small tanks displayed quantities of colored liquids. One end of the chamber was given to a low console, with adjuncts which Etzwane assumed to be controls. On the padded bench beside the controls rested three asutra. At Etzwane's entry, they shrank back against the transparent dome, hissing in shock. One produced a small black mechanism which spat lavender fire towards Etzwane. He had already flung himself aside; the fire struck into the Alula at his back. Etzwane could not use his energy gun for fear of rupturing the dome; he lunged, jerking and ducking across the room. One of the asutra scuttled into a small passageway, no more than a foot square; Etzwane smashed the second creature with the flat of his blade. The third sidled, hissing and whistling, to the bank of controls. Etzwane seized it and threw it into the center of the room, where the Alula stamped it to pulp.

The man who had been struck by the bolt lay staring up through the low dome at the stars; he was dying and nothing could be done for him. Etzwane ordered two men to remain on guard; they gave him truculent stares, challenging his authority. Etzwane ignored their recalcitrance. 'Take care; do not stand where an asutra can aim at you from that little passage yonder. Block off the opening if you can. Be alert!' He departed the room and went off after Karazan.

A ramp led down to a central hold, and here lay the captives from Caraz, drugged and torpid, on shelves which radiated from the walls like the spokes of a wheel. Karazan had killed one of the lumpish gray attendants; two more stood submissively to the side. None of the three carried asutras. In all, two hundred men, women, and children lay stacked like billets of timber and among them Karazan stood in the center of the room, scowling uncertainly from the gray host-creatures to the captives, at a loss, perhaps for the first time in his life.

'These people are well enough as they are,' Etzwane told Karazan. 'Let them sleep. Another matter is more urgent. The asutra have small passages where at least one has taken refuge. We must search the ship, taking great precautions, for the creatures carry energy weapons; already they have killed one man. Our best advantage is to block off the passages as we come to them, until we learn the plan of the ship.'

Karazan said, 'It is smaller than I had expected; not a comfortable or easy place to be.'

'The asutra have built as close to their own scale as possible. With luck we shall soon be back down on the surface. Until then we can only wait and hope that the asutra can't call for help.'

Karazan blinked. 'How could they do that?'

'The advanced races talk through empty space, using the power of lightning.'

'Preposterous,' muttered Karazan, looking around the chamber. 'Why, in the first place, should they go to such lengths for slaves? They have the toad-things, the black monsters like your captive, the red demons, and who knows how many other servants?'

'Nothing about the asutra is certain,' said Etzwane. 'One guess is as good as another. Perhaps each of their hosts serves a special function. Perhaps they simply enjoy a variety of hosts.'

'No matter,' growled Karazan, 'we must dig them out of their crannies.' He called instructions to his men and sent them off in pairs. Declaring himself too cumbersome to aid in the search, he took the gray creatures to the observation dome and tried to persuade them to take the ship down to Durdane, without success. Etzwane went off to examine the lift car, still in its socket, and could discover no means to control it. He next searched for food and water, which he found in bins and tanks under the slave hold. The atmosphere seemed fresh; somewhere aboard the ship an automatic renewal system was at work, and Etzwane hoped that if asutra were alive and in hiding they would not think to stifle the intruders. What, in a similar position, would he do himself? If a transfer ship were due from the home-world, he would do nothing, but allow the problem to be solved by exterior means . . . Two by two the Alul warriors came to report. They had discovered the drive system, the energy generators, the air-purification system. They had surprised and killed one asutra riding the neck of his gray host, but had encountered no others; in a dozen areas they had blocked off asutra passages. Etzwane, now with nothing better to do, made a slow exploration of the ship, trying to learn the location of the asutra refuge. In this work he was assisted by the Alula, who had gained a measure of confidence.

For hours the group studied the ship, estimating distances and volumes, and finally concluded that the private refuge of the asutra lay directly under the control dome, in a space about ten feet square and four feet high. Etzwane and Karazan examined the outside of this space and wondered if they could break in. The walls showed no seams and were formed of a material unknown to Etzwane: neither glass nor metal. The space, Etzwane theorised, constituted the private quarters of the asutra, and he wondered how long they could survive without nourishment – though of course there might be nutriment within the space.

Dawn approached. Durdane was a great black-purple disk surrounded by stars, with a pulsing magenta flare in the east. Blue Etta swung over the horizon, then came pink Sasetta, and finally white Zael, and the face of Durdane awoke to the light.

The ship hung above Caraz, at a distance which Etzwane estimated to be about two hundred miles. Below would be Shagfe village, too inconsequential to be noticed. From south to north extended the Caraz rivers, enormous silver-purple snakes, languid on crumpled plush. In the far southwest was Lake Nior and a line of smaller lakes. Etzwane speculated as to the force which held the depot ship in place, and how long it might take to fall to the surface if the asutra cut off the power. Etzwane winced, imagining the last few seconds . . . Still, the asutra had nothing to gain by destroying their ship. Etzwane reflected upon the curious similarities among creatures as disparate as man, asutra, Roguskhoi, and Ka. All needed sustenance and shelter, all used light to locate themselves spatially . . . To communicate all used sound, rather than light or touch or odor, for simple and universal reasons. Sound pervaded and filled an area; sound could be produced with minimal energy; sound was infinitely flexible. Telepathy? A faculty unevenly useful to a man but perhaps employed more consistently by other species; indeed, to regard a faculty so basic as restricted to the human race would be irrational. The study and comparison of intelligent life-forms must be a fascinating endeavor, thought Etzwane . . . He scanned the sky in all directions, which was dead black and blazing with stars. Much too early to expect Ifness and an Earth ship. But not too early to fear the coming of an asutra vessel. The depot ship itself was a squat cylinder, studded at twenty-foot intervals with thick cones ending in white-metal radiants. The skin, Etzwane noted, was not the copper of the ships he had previously seen, but a burnished gray-black, on which shone oily lusters of crimson, dark blue, and green. Etzwane went once more to study the controls. No doubt but that these were in principal similar to the controls of an Earth ship, and he suspected that Ifness, had he been allowed the opportunity, might have puzzled out the functions of the odd little fingers and knobs and tanks of gray jelly . . . Karazan appeared from below. Claustrophobia had made him edgy and irritable; only in the observation dome, with unobstructed space surrounding him, did he tend to relax. 'I cannot break the wall. Our knives and clubs are unequal to the task, and I cannot understand the asutra tools.'

'I don't see how they can menace us,' Etzwane reflected, 'provided that all the passages are blocked. If they became desperate they could possibly burn their way out and attack us with their guns . . . If they would lower us to the ground they could go their way, in spite of Ifness' yearning for a spaceship, which he can procure at some other time.'

'I agree in every respect,' said Karazan. 'I dislike this

hanging in mid-air like a bird in a cage. If we could make the creatures understand us, no doubt an accommodation could be arranged. Why not try once more with the toad-men? We have nothing better to do.'

They went down to the slave hold, where the toad-men crouched in apathy. Etzwane led one of them to the observation dome, and by dint of gestures towards the controls and down at the surface, indicated that the creature should lower the vessel to the ground – but to no avail; the gray thing stood staring in all directions, the palps rising and falling at its breathing orifices in evidence of some unknowable emotion.

Etzwane went so far as to push the creature towards the controls; it became rigid and exuded a foul-smelling slime from glands down its dorsal ridge. Etzwane desisted from his efforts.

After a half hour of cogitation he went to the blocked-off asutra passage and cautiously removed the sacks of cereal cake stopping the aperture. He hissed and whistled in as conciliatory a manner as he could contrive, then listened. No sound, no response. He tried again, and waited. Again without success. Etzwane closed off the hole once more, irritated and disappointed. The asutra, with intelligence at least equivalent to the human, ought to have recognised that Etzwane was offering a truce.

Etzwane went to look down at Durdane, now fully exposed to the sunlight. Lake Nior had become obscured under a swirl of cirrus; the ground directly below was likewise hidden . . . The asutra's refusal to respond suggested an inability to compromise or cooperate. The creature seemed to expect no quarter and assuredly would give none. Etzwane remembered the Roguskhoi and the horrors they had worked upon the folk of Shant. According to previous assumptions, the Roguskhoi had been an experimental weapon designed for use against the Earth worlds, but now it seemed likely that the asutra had the creatures of the black globe-ships in mind . . . Etzwane scowled down at Durdane. A situation which became ever more mysterious and contradictory. He mustered in his mind those questions which at one time or another had caused him perplexity. Why did the asutra trouble with human slaves when the Ka were equally deft, strong, and agile? Why had the Ka destroyed Hozman's asutra with such passion? How could the asutra hope to match the Roguskhoi against a technically proficient race? And another matter: when the Ka had been trapped in the wrecked spaceship, why had not the asutra escaped, as it easily could have done? Curious matters! Which might or might not at some time be illuminated.

The day dragged past. The men ate rations of the dried meat they had carried with them and cautiously sampled the asutra cereal cake, which proved bland but not unpleasant. The sooner Ifness arrived with a rescue ship the better. Ifness would come, of this Etzwane felt certain. Ifness had never failed in any undertaking; Ifness was too proud a man to tolerate failure . . . Etzwane went down to the slave hold and looked along the pale, still faces. He found Rune the Willow Wand and stood for several minutes examining the even features. He touched her neck, feeling for a pulse, but was confused by the throb of his own heart. It would be pleasant indeed to ride the plains of Caraz alone with Rune. Slowly, reluctantly, he turned away. He wandered around the ship, marveling at the precise workmanship and the expert engineering. What a miracle was a spaceship, which effortlessly could take thinking creatures such vast distances!

Etzwane went back to the dome and gazed in helpless fascination at the controls . . . The suns sank; night concealed the world below.

Night passed; day came, to reveal Hozman Sore-throat

sprawled face down at the back of the slave racks, a cord tight around his neck and his tongue lolling forth. Karazan muttered in disapproval but made no effort to discover the murderers; Hozman's death seemed a matter almost trivial.

The day proceeded. A mood of doubt and uncertainty infected the ship. The zest of victory was gone; the Alula were dispirited . . . Once more Etzwane whistled down the passage for the asutra, with no more success than before. He began to wonder if all the asutra were dead. He had seen one enter the passage, but subsequently an asutra riding on the neck of a toad-thing had been killed; it might have been the same asutra.

The day passed; then another and another. Durdane daily showed a different pattern of clouds; otherwise the scene was static. Etzwane assured the Alula that the very lack of event was a good omen, but Karazan retorted, 'I cannot follow your reasoning. Suppose Ifness were killed on his way to Shillinsk? What if he were unable to communicate with his colleagues? Or assume that they refused to listen to him. What then? Our wait here would feel the same as it does now, and would represent no omen whatever.'

Etzwane tried to explain Ifness' peculiar and perverse personality, but Karazan only made an impatient gesture. 'He is a man, and nothing is certain.'

At this moment a cry came from the lookouts, who stood night and day in the observation dome. 'A spacecraft moves through the sky!'

Etzwane jumped up, heart in his mouth. The time was too early, far too early, to expect Ifness. He peered through the dome to where the lookout pointed . . . High above, a bronze disk-ship slid lazily across the sky, the suns' light reflecting from its skin.

'It is an asutra ship,' said Etzwane.

Karazan said, somewhat heavily, 'We have only one option, and that is to fight. Surprise is once again our ally, for they cannot expect to find the ship in enemy hands.'

Etzwane glanced at the console. Lights blinked and flickered, signifying what, he did not know. If the disk-ship were attempting to communicate and raised no response, it would approach with caution. Surprise was not so great an ally as Karazan had hoped.

The disk curved north, sank at a slant, and halted, to hang quietly a mile away. Then it flickered suddenly green and disappeared. The sky was empty.

From a dozen throats came the hiss of released breath. 'Now why is that?' Karazan demanded of the company in general. 'I am not the man for this sort of business; I detest puzzlement.'

Etzwane shook his head. 'I can only say that I prefer the ship's absence to its company.'

'It realises our presence and plans to catch us napping,' Karazan grumbled. 'We will be ready.'

For the rest of the day all hands crowded the observation dome, save those sent forth to patrol the ship. The bronze disk did not reappear, and presently the group relaxed and conditions were as before.

Four days dragged past. The Alula lapsed into surly taciturnity and the patrols began to lack crispness. Etzwane complained to Karazan, who gave back an inarticulate mutter.

'If discipline deteriorates, we're in trouble,' Etzwane observed. 'We must maintain morale. After all, everybody understood the circumstances before they left Durdane.'

Karazan made no reply, but a short time later he called his men together and issued a set of instructions. 'We are Alula,' he said. 'We are famed for our fortitude. We must demonstrate this quality now. After all, we are suffering nothing more serious than boredom and cramped quarters. The situation might be worse.'

The Alula listened in somber silence and subsequently went about their routines with greater alertness.

Late in the afternoon an event occurred which drastically altered the situation. Etzwane, looking east over the great mulberry-gray expanse, noticed a black sphere hanging motionless in the sky, at a distance impossible to estimate. Etzwane watched for ten minutes while the black globe hung motionless. On sudden thought he looked down to the control panel, to notice lights blinking and altering color. Karazan entered the compartment; Etzwane pointed out the black globe. Karazan asked in a wistful voice. 'Could it be the Earth ship, to carry us down to the soil?'

'Not yet. Ifness said two weeks at the earliest; the time is too soon.'

'Then what ship flies yonder? Another asutra ship?'

'I told you of the battle at Thrie Orgai,' said Etzwane. 'I would suppose this to be a ship of the asutra's enemies, the people of mystery.'

'As the ship is approaching,' Karazan noted, 'the mystery is about to be elucidated.'

The black ship curved down at a slant, passing a mile south of the depot; it slowed and drifted to a halt. At precisely the point where it had disappeared, the bronze-copper disk-ship materialised with venomous stealth. For an instant it lay quiescent, then spurted forth a pair of projectiles. The black globe, as if by nervous reflex, discharged countermissiles; midway between the ships a soundless dazzle blotted out the sky. Etzwane and Karazan would have been blinded except for the stuff of the dome which resisted the surge of light.

The bronze disk had focused four jets of energy on the black globe, which glowed red and burned open: apparently its protective system had failed. In retaliation it projected a gush of purple flame, which for an instant flared over the disk-ship like the blast of a torch; then the flame flickered and died. The black globe rolled over like a dead fish. The disk fired another projectile; it struck into the hole burnt by the converging beams. The globe exploded and Etzwane received an instantaneous image of black fragments flying away from a core of lambent material; among the stuff he thought to glimpse hurtling corpses, grotesquely sprawled and rotating. Fragments struck the depot ship, clanging, jarring, sending vibrations through the hull.

The sky was again clear and open. Of the black globe, not an element remained; the bronze disk had disappeared.

Etzwane said in a hollow voice, 'The disk-ship lies in ambush. The depot is bait. The asutra know we are here; they believe us to be their enemies and they wait for our ships to arrive.'

Etzwane and Karazan searched the sky with a new anxiety. The simple rescue of four girls from Hozman Sore-throat had expanded into a situation far past all their imaginings. Etzwane had not bargained for participation in a space war; Karazan and the Alula had not comprehended the psychological pressures which would be put upon them.

The sky remained clear of traffic; the suns sank at the back of a million magenta cloud-feathers. Night was instant; dusk showed only as a sad, subtle bloom upon the face of Durdane.

During the night the patrols were relaxed, to Etzwane's displeasure. He complained to Karazan, pointing out that conditions remained as before, but Karazan reacted with an irritable sweep of his great arm, consigning Etzwane and his peevish little fears to oblivion. Karazan and the

Alula had become demoralised, Etzwane angrily told himself, to such an extent that they would have welcomed attack, captivity, slavery, anything which might have provided them with a palpable antagonist. Pointless to harangue them, Etzwane brooded; they no longer listened.

Night passed, and the day and other nights and days. The Alula sat huddled in the observation dome; they stared out at the sky, seeing nothing. The time had arrived when Ifness might be expected; but no one any longer believed in Ifness nor the Earth ship; the only reality was the sky cage and the empty panorama.

Etzwane had considered a dozen systems for warning Ifness, should he indeed arrive, and had rejected them all, or, more properly, none was in any degree workable. Presently Etzwane himself lost count of the days. The presence of the other men had long since grown odious, but apathy was a stronger force than hostility, and the men suffered each other in a silent community of mutual detestation.

Then the quality of the waiting changed, and became a sense of imminence. The men muttered uneasily and watched from the observation dome, the whites of their eyes showing. Everyone knew that something was about to occur, and soon, and this was the case. The bronze disk-ship reappeared.

The men aboard the depot gave soft guttural groans of despair; Etzwane made a last wild inspection of the sky, willing the Earth ships into existence. Where was Ifness?

The sky was vacant except for the bronze disk-ship. It eased in a circle around the depot, then halted and slowly approached. It loomed enormous, blotting out the sky. The hulls touched; the depot jerked and quivered. From the location of the entry port came a throbbing sound. Karazan looked at Etzwane. 'They are coming aboard. You have your energy weapon; will you fight?'

Etzwane gave his head a dreary shake. 'Dead we are no use to anyone, least of all ourselves.'

Karazan sneered. 'So it is to be surrender? They will take us away and make us their slaves.'

'This is the prospect,' said Etzwane. 'It is better than death. Our hope is that the Earth worlds at last know the situation and will intervene on our behalf.'

Karazan gave a jeering laugh and clenched his great fists, but still stood indecisive. From below came the sounds of ingress. Karazan told his warriors: 'Make no resistance. Our force falls short of our desires. We must suffer the penalties of weakness.'

Into the dome ran two black Ka, each with an asutra clamped to the nape of its neck. They ignored the men except to shoulder them aside and moved to the controls. One worked the curious little studs with ease and certainty. Deep within the ship an engine whined. The view outside the dome grew dim, then dark; nothing could be seen. Another Ka came to the entrance of the dome. It made gestures, indicating that the Alula and Etzwane were to leave. Suddenly Karazan hunched to the exit, and bending his neck, marched down the ramp towards the slave hold. Etzwane followed, and the others came behind.

Chapter 8

The Alula squatted in the aisles between the slave racks. The Ka ignored them as they moved about their tasks, asutra clamped to their necks like leeches.

The depot ship was in motion. The men felt no vibration, no lunge or surge, but the knowledge was sure, as if the shifting infrasubstance rasped upon a sensitive area of the brain. The men huddled silently, each thinking his own sullen thoughts. The Ka paid them no heed.

Time passed, at a pace impossible to measure. Where uncertainty and taut nerves had previously drawn out the hours, now a dismal melancholy worked to the same effect.

Etzwane's single hope was that Ifness had not been killed on the Plain of Blue Flowers, and that vanity would impel him to their assistance. The Alula knew no hope whatever and were apathetic. Etzwane looked across the chamber to the niche where lay Rune the Willow Wand. He could see the outline of her temple and cheekbone, and felt a sudden warmth. To seem gallant in her sight, he had risked and lost his freedom. Such would be Ifness' insulting opinion. Was it justified? Etzwane heaved a sad sigh. His motives had been complex; he did not know them himself.

Karazan heaved himself to his feet. He stood motionless for ten seconds, then stretched out his great arms, twisted them this way and that, making the muscles writhe. Etzwane became alarmed; Karazan's face was peculiarly calm and intent. The Alula watched, interested but indifferent. Etzwane jumped up, called out sharply. Karazan gave no signal that he had heard. Etzwane shook his shoulder; Karazan slowly turned his head; Etzwane saw no expression in the wide gray eyes.

The other Alula rose to their feet. One muttered to Etzwane, 'Stand back. He is in death-seek.'

Another said, 'It is dangerous to molest folk in this condition; after all, his way may be the best.'

'Not so!' cried Etzwane. 'Dead folk are no good to anyone. Karazan!' He shook the massive shoulders. 'Listen! Do you hear me? If you ever want to see Lake Nior again, listen!'

He thought that a flicker of response appeared in Karazan's eyes. 'We are not without hope! Ifness is alive; he will find us.'

One of the other Alula asked anxiously, 'Do you really believe this?'

'If you knew Ifness you would never doubt it! The man cannot tolerate defeat.'

'This may be,' said the Alula, 'but how does this avail when we are lost upon a far star?'

From Karazan's throat came a hoarse sound and then words. 'How can he find us?'

'I don't know,' Etzwane admitted, 'but I will never lose hope.'

Karazan said in a throbbing voice, 'It is foolish to speak of hope. In vain did you draw me back.'

'If you are a brave man you will hope,' said Etzwane. ' "Death-seek" is the easy way.'

Karazan made no reply. Once more he seated himself, then stretching out full-length he slept. The other Alula muttered together, turning cool glances towards Etzwane, as if his interference with Karazan's 'death-seek' were not to their liking . . . Etzwane went to his accustomed place and presently fell asleep.

The Alula had become unfriendly. Pointedly they ignored Etzwane and pitched their voices so that he could not hear. Karazan did not share the hostility, but sat off by himself, twirling a weighted thong around his finger.

The next time Etzwane slept, he awoke suddenly to find three Alula standing over him: Black Hulanik, Fairo the Handsome, Ganim Thornbranch. Ganim Thornbranch carried a length of cord. Etzwane sat up, energy gun ready at hand. He remembered Hozman Sore-throat and his lolling tongue. The Alula, blank-faced, moved off across the room.

Etzwane reflected a few moments, then went to Karazan. 'Some of your men were about to kill me.'

Karazan nodded ponderously and twirled his thong.

'What is the reason for this?'

It seemed that Karazan might make no response. Then, with something of an effort, he said, 'There is no particular reason. They want to kill someone and have selected you. It is a game of sorts.'

'I don't care to join,' Etzwane declared in a brassy voice. 'They can play with someone from their own group. Order them to let me be.'

Karazan shrugged lethargically. 'It makes little difference.'

'Not to you. To me it makes a great deal of difference.'

Karazan shrugged and twirled his thong.

Etzwane went off to consider the situation. So long as he remained awake, he would live. When he slept, he would die – perhaps not the first, nor even the second time. They would play with him, try to break his nerve. Why? No reason. A game, the malicious sport of a barbarian tribe. Cruelty? Etzwane was the outsider, a non-Alula with no more status than a chumpa captured for the baiting.

Several recourses suggested themselves. He could shoot his tormentors and abate the nuisance once and for all. A solution not wholly satisfactory. Even if the asutra failed to confiscate the gun, the game would continue in a more vicious form, with everyone waiting until he slept. The best defense was offense, thought Etzwane. He rose to his feet and crossed the chamber, as if on his way to the latrine. His eyes fell on the still form of Rune the Willow Wand; she seemed less appealing than before; she was, after all, an Alul barbarian, no better than her fellows . . . Etzwane turned aside to the room containing the bags of meal cake and the water tanks. In the doorway he halted to inspect the group. They looked back askance. Smiling grimly Etzwane brought forward a case of food and seated himself. The Alula watched with alert but expressionless faces. Etzwane once more rose to his feet. He took a wafer of the meal cake and a mug of water. Reseating himself, he ate and drank. He noticed several of the Alula licking their lips. As if by common impulse, all turned away and somewhat ostentatiously gave themselves to slumber.

Karazan looked on soberly, his noble forehead creased in a frown. Etzwane ignored him. What if Karazan wanted food and drink? Etzwane had come to no firm decision. He would probably provide Karazan his sustenance.

Upon consideration he moved back into the shadows, where he was less vulnerable to a thrown knife: the obvious response of the Alula. Presently, dissatisfied with his arangements, he stacked several boxes of meal to provide a barricade behind which he could see but not be seen.

He began to feel drowsy. His eyelids sagged . . . He awoke with a start to notice one of the Alula sidling close.

'Two more steps and you're a dead man,' said Etzwane.

The Alula stopped short. 'Why should you deny me water? I took no part in the baiting.'

'You did nothing to control the three who did. Starve and thirst in their company – until they are dead.'

'This is not fair! You do not reckon with our customs.'

'To the contrary. It is now I who do the baiting. When Fairo the Handsome, Ganim Thornbranch, and Black Hulanik are dead, you shall drink.'

The thirsty Alula turned slowly away. Karazan intoned, 'It is an ill thing which has occurred.'

'You might have stopped it,' said Etzwane. 'You chose to do nothing.'

Rising to his feet Karazan glared into the provisions locker; for a moment he seemed the Karazan of old. Then his shoulders slumped. He said, 'This is true. I gave no instructions; why worry about one death when all are doomed?'

'I happen to worry about my death,' said Etzwane. 'And now I am doing the baiting, and the victims are Fairo, Ganim, Hulanik.'

Karazan looked towards the three named men; every eye in the room followed his gaze. The three men made defiant grimaces and glared about them.

Karazan spoke in a conciliatory voice. 'Let us put aside this business; it is unnecessary and unreasonable.'

'Why did you not say this while I was being baited?' demanded Etzwane in a fury. 'When the three are dead you will eat and drink.'

Karazan settled once more to his previous position. Time passed. At first there was an ostentatious show of solidarity with the three, then other groups formed, talking in whispers. The three huddled back between the racks, and their glass knives glittered from the shadows.

Etzwane dozed once more. He awoke, intensely aware of danger. The chamber was still. Etzwane rose to his knees and backed further into the shadows. Across the outer chamber the Alula were watching. Someone had reached the wall and now sidled inch by inch, out of Etzwane's range of vision, towards the provision locker. Who?

Karazan no longer sat by the wall.

A paralysing roar; a vast shape filled the aperture. Etzwane pulled the trigger, more by startlement than design. He saw a star-shaped dazzle as the flame struck into a great face. The lunging man was instantly dead. His body tottered into the wall and fell over backward.

Etzwane came slowly out into the room, which was hushed in horror. He stood looking down at the corpse, wondering what Karazan had intended, for Karazan carried no weapon. He had known Karazan as a large-souled man: simple, direct, and benevolent. Karazan deserved better than his cramped, despairing fate. He looked along the silent white faces. 'The responsibility is yours. You tolerated malice and now you have lost your great leader.'

Among the Alula there was a furtive shifting of position, a secret interchange of glances. Change came so quickly as to numb the mind: from dazed torpor to wild, screaming activity. Etzwane stumbled back against the wall. Alula leapt through the air; there was slashing and hacking and the doing of grisly deeds; and in a moment all was finished. On the deck Fairo, Ganim Thornbranch, Black Hulanik wallowed in their own blood, and two other men as well.

Etzwane said, 'Quick, before the asutra arrive. Drag the bodies into the racks. Find room on the shelves.'

Dead bodies lay beside living. Etzwane broke open a

sack of meal and blotted up the blood. In five minutes the slave hold was orderly and calm, if somewhat less crowded than before. A few minutes later three Ka with asutra peering from the napes of their necks passed through the hold, but did not pause.

The Alula, with hunger and thirst sated and with emotions spent, fell into a state of inertness, more stupor than sleep. Etzwane, though distrustful of the unpredictable Alul temperament, decided that vigilance would only foster a new hostility and gave himself up to sleep, first taking the precaution of tying the energy gun to a loop of his pouch.

He slept undisturbed. When at last he awoke, he realized that the ship was at rest.

Chapter 9

The air in the hold seemed stale; the bluish illumination had dimmed and was more depressing than ever. From overhead came the thud of footsteps and fluctuating snatches of nasal Ka warbling. Etzwane rose to his feet and went to the ramp to listen. The Alula also rose and stood looking uncertainly towards the ramp: a far cry from the swaggering warriors Etzwane had met an aeon before at a bend of the Vurush River.

A grinding hiss, a chatter of ratchets: a section of wall drew back; a wash of gray light flooded the hold, to drown the blue glow.

Etzwane pushed past the Alula, where he could look out the opening. He leaned back in dismay and shock, unable to find meaning in the welter of strange shapes and colors. He looked once more through narrowed eyes, matching the pattern-forming capabilities of his mind against the alien stuff, and aspects of the landscape shifted into mental focus. He saw steep-sided sugarloaf hills overgrown with a lustrous black, dark-green, and brown pelt of vegetation. Beyond and above spread a heavy gray overcast, under which hung pillows of black cloud and a few veils of rain. Along the lower slopes straggled lines of irregular structures, built from rough lumps of an oyster-white material. At ground level the structures formed a denser complex. Most were built of the pallid lumps; a few seemed monolithic forms of black scoriaceous slag. Passages wound between and around, slanting and curving, without apparent purpose. Certain of these were smooth and wide and carried vehicles: cage-like drays; wagons, resembling beetles with raised wings; smaller lizard-like vehicles, darting inches above the surface. At intervals posts held up enormous black rectangles, lacking marks or discernible purpose. Etzwane wondered whether the eyes of Ka and asutra distinguished colors invisible to himself. The immediate foreground was a flat, paved area surrounded by a fence of woven bronze. Etzwane, who by instinct observed and interpreted colors automatically, after the symbology of Shant, noted no purposeful use of color. Somewhere in the confusion of size, form, and proportion, he thought, symbology must exist; technical civilisation was impossible without control over abstractions.

The inhabitants of the place were Ka, at least half of whom carried asutra on their necks. No gray toad-men were in evidence, nor were human beings to be seen.

Except one. Into the slave hold climbed a person tall and spare, in a shapeless, coarse-fibered cloak. Stiff gray hair lay piled above the seamed gray face like a forkful of hay; the chin was long and without hair. Etzwane saw that the person was a woman, though her aspect and conduct were asexual. She called in a loud, windy voice, 'The persons now awake; follow me to the ground! Smartly now, quick and easy. This is the first thing to know; never wait for two commands.' The woman spoke a dialect barely comprehensible; she seemed bitter and wild and grim as a winter storm. She set off down the ramp. Etzwane gingerly followed, glad to win free from the detested slave hold and its nightmare memories.

The group descended to the paved area under the great black depot ship. On a walkway above stood four Ka, looming like dark statues with asutra at their necks. The woman led them into the mouth of a fenced run. 'Wait here; I go to wake the sleepers.'

An hour passed. The men stood hunched against the fence, glum and silent. Etzwane, clinging to his Ifness-inspired shred of faith, was able to take a melancholy interest in the surroundings. The passage of time made the circumstances no less strange. From various directions came the muffled Ka fluting, mingled with the hiss of traffic on the road immediately across the fence. Etzwane watched the eight-wheeled, segmented drays roll past. Who guided them? He could see no cab or compartment other than a small cupola at the front, and within a small dark mass: asutra . . . From the depot ship marched the woman followed by dazed folk who had occupied the shelves. They stumbled and limped and looked here and there in sad amazement. Etzwane noted Srenka and presently Gulshe; the erstwhile bravos hunched along as miserably as the others. Gulshe's gaze passed across Etzwane's face; he gave no signal of recognition. At the end of the procession came Rune the Willow Wand, and she as well looked past Etzwane without interest.

'Halt!' cried the lead woman in her great coarse voice. 'Here we wait for the omnibus. Now let me speak to you. Your old life is gone and irretrievably; this is the world Kahei and you are like fresh-born babes with another life ahead. It is not too bad unless they take you for testing, and then it is death. Still, who lives forever? In the meanwhile, you will never hunger or thirst or lack shelter, and life is tolerable. The men and agile women will be trained to fight in the war, and it is pointless to claim no part in the quarrel or think to avoid battle against men like yourselves; this is the fact and you must do the requirement.

'Waste nothing on grief; it is the easy way and the futile way. Should you wish to breed, make application to one or another intercessor, and a suitable partner will be assigned.

'Insubordination, lagging and loitering, fighting and mischievousness, all are forbidden; penalties are not graduated, but in all cases absolute. The omnibus is here. Climb up the ramp and step to the forward end.'

Crowded on the omnibus, Etzwane could see little of the passing countryside. The road led parallel to the hills for a space, then swung off across a plain. Occasionally a cluster of lumpy gray towers stood against the sky; a velvety growth of moss, dark red, dark green, or violet-black, covered the ground.

The omnibus halted; the slaves filed out upon a concrete compound, surrounded on three sides by structures of oyster-white lumps. To the north rolled low hills, commanded by a landmark crag of rotten basalt. To the east spread a vast black quagmire, disappearing at the horizon into the gloom of the sky. Nearby, at the edge of the compound, rested a bronze disk-ship, all ports open and ramps down upon the concrete. Etzwane thought he recognised the ship as that which had evacuated the Roguskhoi chieftains from the Engh Valley in Palasedra.

The slaves were herded to a barracks. Along the way they passed a set of long, narrow pens exhaling a vile stench. In some of the pens wandered andromorphs of several freakish varieties. Etzwane noticed a dozen Roguskhoi. Another group verged towards the Ka. In one pen huddled half a dozen spindly creatures with Ka torsos and grotesque simulations of the human head. Behind the pens ran a long low shed: the laboratory, so Etzwane realised, where these biological anomalies were created. After years of speculation he had learned the source of the Roguskhoi.

*

The captives were separated, men from women, then divided into platoons of eight persons. To each platoon was assigned a corporal drawn from a cadre of the captives already on the scene. To Etzwane's group came an old man, thin, gaunt, seamed as the bark of an old tree, but none the less muscular and incessantly active, all elbows and sharp knees.

'My name is Polovits,' declared the old man. 'The first lesson you must learn, and learn well, is obedience, quick and absolute, because no second chance is offered. The masters are decisive. They do not punish, they destroy. A war is in progress: they fight a strong enemy and have no inclination towards clemency. I remind you once more: to every instruction give smart and scrupulous obedience, or you will not live to receive another order. In the next few days you will see my statements exemplified. There is generally a depletion of one third in the first month; if you value life, obey all orders without hesitation.

'The rules of the cantonment are not complicated. You may not fight. I will adjudicate quarrels, and my judgment is final. You may not sing, shout, or whistle. You may not indulge your sexual desires without prior arrangement. You must be tidy; disorder is not tolerated. There are two principal roads to advancement. First, zeal. A dedicated man will become a corporal. Second, communication. If you learn the Great Song, you will gain valuable privileges, for very few persons can sing with the Ka. It is difficult, as those who try will discover, but fighting in the first rank is worse.'

Etzwane said, 'I have a question. Whom must we fight?'

'Ask no idle questions,' snapped Polovits. 'It is a useless habit and shows instability. Look at me! I have asked never a question and I have survived on Kahei for long years. I was taken from Shauzade district as a child during the second slavings. I saw the Red Warriors created, and it was a hard time. How many of us survive now? I could count their names in a trice. Why did we survive?' Polovits peered from face to face. 'Why did we want to survive?' Polovits' own face showed a haggard triumph. 'Because we were men! Fate has given us the one life to live, and we use it to the best! I make the same recommendation to you: do your best! Nothing else is valid.'

'You cautioned me in regard to idle questions,' said Etzwane. 'I ask a question which is not idle. Are we offered any inducement? Can we hope to see Durdane again as free men?'

Polovits' voice became hoarse. 'Your inducement is persistence of life! And hope – what is hope? On Durdane there is no hope; death comes for all, and it comes here as well. And freedom? It is at your option here and now. Notice the hills; they are empty. The way is open; go now and be free! No one will halt you. But before you go, take heed! The only food is weed and wort; the only water is mist. You will bloat on the herbs; you will call in vain for water. Freedom is yours.'

Etzwane asked nothing more. Polovits pulled the cloak around his thin shoulders. 'We will now eat. Then we will commence our training.'

To eat, the squad stood up to a long trough containing lukewarm mush, stalks of a crisp, cold vegetable, and spiced pellets. After the meal Polovits put the men through calisthenics, then took them to one of the low, lizardlike vehicles.

'We have been assigned the function of "stealthy attack". These are the strike cars. They move on vibrating pads and are capable of high speed. Each man of the squad will be assigned his car, and he must maintain it with care. It is a dangerous and valuable weapon.'

'I wish to ask a question,' said Etzwane, 'but I am not

sure whether you will consider it "idle". I do not want to be struck dead for simple curiosity.'

Polovits put a stony gaze upon him. 'Curiosity is a futile habit.'

Etzwane held his tongue. Polovits nodded curtly and turned to the lizard-car. 'The driver lies flat, with his arms ahead. He looks down into a prism which shows him an adequate field of view. With arms and legs he controls the motion; with his chin he discharges either his torpedoes or his fire-stab.'

Polovits demonstrated the controls, then took the squad to a set of mock-ups. For three hours the group trained at the simulated controls; there was then a rest-break, then a two-hour demonstration of maintenance techniques which each man would be required to use on his vehicle.

The sky darkened; with twilight came a fine rain. In the dismal gray gloom the squad marched to the barracks. For supper the trough held a bland, sweet soup which the men dipped up with mugs. Polovits then said, 'Who among you wishes to learn the Great Song?'

Etzwane asked, 'What is involved?'

Polovits decided that the question was legitimate. 'The Great Song recounts the history of Kahei through symbolic sounds and sequences. The Ka communicate by singing themes of allusion, and you must do the same through the medium of a double-flute. The language is logical, flexible, and expressive, but difficult to learn.'

'I wish to learn the Great Song,' said Etzwane.

Polovits showed him a harsh grin. 'I thought you would decide as much.' And Etzwane decided that he did not like Polovits. The need for dissembling therefore increased; he must truckle and submit; he must throw himself into the program with apparent zeal.

Polovits seemed to perceive the flow of Etzwane's

thoughts and made a cryptic observation, 'In either case I will be satisfied.'

For a period existence went quietly. The sun – or suns – never appeared; the dank gloom oppressed the spirits and made for dreariness and lethargy. The daily routine included calisthenics, periods of training in the lizard-cars, and work sessions, which might consist of food preparation, sorting of ores, shaping and polishing of swamp wood. Neatness was emphasised. Detachments policed the barracks and groomed the landscape. Etzwane wondered whether the insistence upon order reflected the will of the asutra or the Ka. Probably the Ka, he decided; it was unlikely that the asutra altered the personality of the Ka any more than they had affected Sajarano of Sershan, or Jurjin, or Jerd Finnerack, or Hozman Sore-throat. The asutra dictated policy and monitored conduct; otherwise it seemed to remained aloof from the life of its host.

Asutra were everywhere evident. Perhaps half the Ka carried asutra; mechanisms were guided by asutra, and Polovits spoke in awe of asutra-guided aircraft. The latter two functions seemed somewhat plebeian activity for the asutra, Etzwane reflected, and would indicate that asutra, no less than Ka, men, ahulph, and chumpa, were divided into categories and castes.

At the end of the day, an hour was set aside for hygiene, sexual activity, which was permitted on the floor of a shed between the male and female barracks, and general recreation. The evening rain, occurring soon after light left the sky, put a term to the period, and the slaves went to their barracks, where they slept on mounds of dried moss. As Polovits had asserted, no guards or fences restrained the slaves from flight into the hills. Etzwane learned that on rare occasions a slave did so choose to seek freedom. Sometimes the fugitive was never again seen; as often he returned to camp after three or four days of hunger and thirst and thankfully resumed the routine. According to one rumor, Polovits himself had fled into the hills and upon his return had become the most diligent slave of the camp.

Etzwane saw two men killed. The first, a stout man, disliked calisthenics and thought to outwit his corporal. The second man was Srenka, who ran amok. In both cases a Ka destroyed the offender with a spurt of energy.

The Great Song of Kahei was for Etzwane a labor of love. The instructor was Kretzel, a squat old woman with a face concealed among a hundred folds and wrinkles. Her memory was prodigious, her disposition was easy, and she was always willing to entertain Etzwane with rumors and anecdotes. In her teaching she used a mechanism which reproduced the rasps, croaks, and warbles of the Great Song in its classic form. Kretzel then duplicated the tones on a pair of double-pipes and translated the significance into words. She made it clear that the Song was only incidentally music; that essentially it served as the basic semantic reference to Ka communication and conceptual thinking.

The Song consisted of fourteen thousand cantos, each a construction of thirty-nine to forty-seven phrases.

'What you will learn,' said Kretzel, 'is the simple First Style. The Second employs overtones, trills, and echoes; the Third inverts harmony and for emphasis reverses phrases; the Fourth combines the Second with augmentations and variations; the Fifth suggests rather than propounds. I know only the First, and superficially at that. The Ka use abbreviations, idioms, allusions, double and triple themes. The language is subtle.'

Kretzel was far less rigorous than Polovits. She told all she knew without restraint. Did the asutra use or understand the Song? Kretzel rocked her shoulders indifferently back and forth. 'Why concern yourself? You will never address yourself to the things. But they know the Song. They know everything, and have brought many changes to Kahei.'

Encouraged by the woman's loquacity, Etzwane asked other questions. 'How long have they been here? Where did they come from?'

'All this is made clear in the last seven hundred cantos, which report the tragedy which came to Kahei. This very land, the North Waste, has known many terrible battles. But now we must work, or the Ka will presume sloth.'

Etzwane made himself a set of double-pipes, and as soon as he had subdued his aversion for the Ka musical intervals, which he found unnatural and discordant, he played the first canto of the Great Song with a skill to amaze the old woman. 'Your dexterity is remarkable. Still, you must play accurately. Yes, my old ears are keen! Your tendency is to ornament and warp the phrases into the ways you know. Absolutely wrong! The Great Song becomes gibberish.'

Sexual activity among the slaves was encouraged, but couples were not allowed to form permanent liaisons. Etzwane occasionally saw Rune the Willow Wand across the compound where the women performed their own exercises, and one day during the period of 'free calisthenics' he took the trouble to approach her. She had lost something of her insouciance and nonchalant grace; she looked at him now without cordiality, and Etzwane saw that she failed to recognise him.

'I am Gastel Etzwane,' he told her. 'Do you remember the camp by the Vurush River where I played music and you dared me to knock away your cap?'

Rune's face showed no change of expression. 'What do you want?'

'Sexual activity is not forbidden. If you are so inclined. I will apply to the corporal and specifically request that – '

She cut him short with a gesture. 'I am not so inclined. Do you think I care to bear a child on this dreary gray hell? Go spend yourself on one of the old women, and bring no more blighted souls to life.'

Eztwane expostulated, citing one principle, then another, but Rune's face became progressively harder. At last she turned and walked away. Etzwane somewhat wistfully returned to his calisthenics.

The days dragged by with a slowness Etzwane found maddening. He estimated their duration to be four or five hours longer than the days of Shant: a situation which upset his natural rhythms and made him alternatively morose and nervously irritable. He learned the first twelve cantos of the Song, both the melodies and the associated significances. He began to practice basic communication, selecting and joining musical phrases. His dexterity was counterbalanced by an almost uncontrollable tendency to play notes and phrases as personal music, slurring here, extending there, inserting gracenotes and trills, until old Kretzel threw up her hands in exasperation. 'The sequence goes thus and so,' and she demonstrated. 'No more, no less! It conveys the idea of a vain search for crayfish along the shore of the Ocean Quagmire during the morning rain. You introduce random elements of other cantos to create a mishmash, a farrago of ideas. Each note must be just, neither under- nor over-blown! Otherwise you sing absurdities!'

Etzwane controlled his fingers and played the themes precisely as Kretzel had indicated. 'Good!' she declared. 'Now we proceed to the next canto, where proto-Ka, the Hiana, cross the mud flats and are annoyed by chirping insects.'

Etzwane much preferred Kretzel's company to the peevish admonitions of Polovits, and he would have spent all his waking hours practicing the Great Song had she allowed. 'Such diligence is wasted,' said Kretzel. 'I know the cantos; I can sing to the black ones in faltering First Style. This is all I can teach you. If you lived a hundred years you might begin to play Second Style, but never could you know the feeling, for you are not a Ka. Then there are Third, Fourth, and Fifth, and then the idioms and cursive forms, the converging and diverging harmonics, the antichords, the stops, the hisses and slurs. Life is too short; why exert yourself?'

Etzwane decided, none the less, to learn as best he could; he had nothing better to do with his time. Every day he found Polovits more detestable, and his only escape was to Kretzel. Or freedom in the hills. According to Polovits, the wilderness afforded neither food nor water, and Kretzel corroborated as much. His best hope of evading Polovits lay in the Great Song . . . What of Ifness? The name seldom occurred to Etzwane. His old life was vague; by the day it dwindled and lost detail. Reality was Kahei; here alone was life. Sooner or later Ifness would appear; sooner or later there would be a rescue – so Etzwane told himself, but every day the idea became more and more abstract.

One afternoon Kretzel became bored with the Song. Complaining of cankerous gums she threw the pipes to a shelf. 'Let them kill me; what difference does it make? I am too old to fight; I know the Song, so they stay my death, and I do not care; my bones will never know the soil of Durdane. You are young; you have hopes. One by one they will go, and nothing will be left but the bare fact of life. Then you will discover the transcendent value of life alone . . . We have been through much hardship; we have known cruel times. When I was young they bred their copper warriors and trained them to spawn in human women, for what purpose I never knew.'

Etzwane said, 'I know well enough. The Roguskhoi were sent to Durdane. They devastated Shant and several great districts of Caraz. Is it not strange? They destroy the folk of Durdane, and at the same time capture them to use as slave warriors against their enemy.'

'It is only another experiment,' said Kretzel wisely. 'The Red Warriors failed, now they try a new weapon for their war.' She peered over her shoulder. 'Take your pipes and play the Song. Polovits watches for slackness. Take heed of Polovits; he likes to kill.' She reached for her own pipes. 'Ah, my poor, tortured gums! This is the nineteenth canto. The Sah and Aianu use raho fibers to wind rope and dig coral nut with blackwood sticks. You will hear both the schemes for blackwood and for rough wood employed in a rude scratching action, as is general usage. But you must carefully play the little-finger flutter, else the scheme is "visiting a place where the quagmire may be distantly seen" from Canto 9635.'

Etzwane played the pipes, watching Polovits from the corner of his eye. Polovits paused to listen, then turned Etzwane a flinty glance and continued on his way.

Later in the day, during calisthenics, Polovits suddenly exploded into fury: 'Crisply then! Do you detest exertion so much that you cannot put your hand to the ground? Never fear, I am watching, and your life is as fragile as a moth-shell. Why do you stand like a post?'

'I await new orders, Corporal Polovits.'

'Your kind is the most venomous, always with a glib retort just short of insolence! Don't indulge in dreams of glory, my Song-playing virtuoso, you won't evade the worst of it! I assure you of this! So now: a hundred high leaps, for your health's sake; let them be agile, with a fine twinkling of the heels!'

In calmness and gravity Etzwane obeyed as best he could. Polovits watched with grim intentness, but could find no fault with the efforts. At last he turned and strode away. With a faint smile on his face, Etzwane returned to Kretzel's little office and practiced the nineteen cantos he already knew and learned the melody to cantos Twenty and Twenty-one from the reproducing machine. He would discover the semantic significance in due course.

Etzwane conducted himself with care, but Polovits was unrelenting. Etzwane's patience wore thin, and he decided to take positive action. Polovits, by some uncanny means, divined the fact of the decision and thrust his angular old face close to Etzwane's. 'A dozen men have thought to best me, and can you guess where they lie at this moment? In the great hole. I know tricks you never heard of! I'm just waiting for a single insurbordinate move, then you will learn the folly of proud attitudes on this sad world Kahei.'

Etzwane had no choice by hypocrisy. He said politely, 'I'm sorry if I have given offense; I want only to remain inconspicuous. Needless to say, I am not here by my own choice.'

'You waste my time with your witticisms,' bawled Polovits. 'I intend to hear no more!' He strode away, and Etzwane went to practice the Song.

Kretzel inquired as to his lack of zest, and Etzwane explained that Polovits was about to take his life. Kretzel gave a whinny of shrill laughter. 'That spleenful little dingbat; he's not worth the rumble of an ahulph's gut! He won't give you to death, because he's afraid to speak a lie. Do you think the Ka are fools? Come, I will teach you Canto 2023, wherein the stave-cutters kill a stone-roller because he dented their moss. Then you need only play the eleventh phrase should Polovits so much as raise a finger. Better! Tell old Polovits that you are rehearsing the Canto of Open Inspection, and that you consider his conduct slack. To work. Polovits is of no more consequence than a bad smell.'

'Gastel Etzwane,' said Polovits, during the morning calisthenics. 'You move with the grace and agility of a pregnant grampus. I cannot accept those kneebands as accomplished facts. Has your well-known musical virtuosity rendered you absentminded? Well, then, answer! I count your silence an insolence. How long must I suffer your slights?'

'Not long at all,' said Etzwane. 'Yonder walks a Monitor; summon him. By chance I have here my pipes and I will play the Canto of Open Inspection, and we shall have justice.'

Polovits' eyes seemed to burn red. His mouth slowly opened, then snapped shut. He swung around and made as if to summon the Ka. As if by great effort he restrained himself. 'So then: he takes you and half this band of club-footed cretins to the hole; how do I gain? I only must start again with a group as bad. We are wasting time! Back to the calisthenics; once again the kneebends. Smartly now!' But Polovits spoke somewhat pensively and refused to meet Etzwane's gaze.

Kretzel asked Etzwane, 'How is Polovits now?'

'He is a changed man,' said Etzwane. 'His tirades have ended, and likewise his tantrums; he is now as meek as a grass-tit, and the drills are almost a pleasure.'

Kretzel was silent and Etzwane once again took up the pipes. He noticed a tear rolling down the brown folds of

Kretzel's cheek, and lowered the pipes. 'Has something occurred to distress you?'

Kretzel rubbed at her face. 'I never think of home; I would long since have been dead had I mourned. But one word stirred a memory and brought it to life; and I thought of the meadows above the Elshuka Pond where my family held a steading. The grass was high, and when I was a little girl I worked long burrows through the grass and surprised two tits at their nesting . . . One day I burrowed a long tunnel through the grass. When it broke open I looked up into the face of Molsk the Man-taker. He took me away in a sack and I never again saw the Elshuka Pond . . . I have no great time to live. They will mix my bones into this sour black soil, when I would once again be home in the sunlight.'

Etzwane blew a pensive tune on the pipes. 'Were many slaves on Kahei when you came?'

'We were among the first. They used us to build their Roguskhoi. I evaded the worst of it when I learned the Song. But the others are gone, save a few. Old Polovits, for one.'

'And in all this time has no one escaped?'

' "Escaped"? To where? The world is a prison!'

'I could take pleasure in doing general harm, if I were able.'

Kretzel gave an indifferent shrug. 'Once I felt the same way, but now – I have played the Great Song too many times. I feel almost a Ka.'

Etzwane recalled the occasion at Shagfe when the Ka captive had destroyed Hozman Sore-throat's asutra. What had triggered this spasm of violence? If all the Ka of Kahei could feel the same impulse, there would be no more asutra. Etzwane became conscious of how little he in fact knew of the Ka, of their way of life, their innate character. He put questions to Kretzel, who at once became cross and advised that he apply himself to the Great Song.

Etzwane said, 'I know twenty-two cantos; there are more than fourteen thousand yet to be learned; I will be an old man before my questions are answered.'

'And I will be dead,' snapped Kretzel. 'So then, attend to the mechanism; hear the double quaver at the end of the second phrase. This is a common device and signifies what is called "vehement assertion". The Ka are a brave and desperate people; their history is a series of tragic plights, and the double quaver expresses this mood, the challenge flung into the face of destiny.'

Polovits, the furious old fighting-cock, with startling abruptness had become a surly introvert, who gave minimum effort to the drills. The tension created by his old antagonism had collapsed; the drills became periods of droning boredom.

The mood, for Etzwane, infected every aspect of existence; he began to feel a disassociation, a sense of existence on two levels, inner and outer, and his mind, retreating into a subjective middle distance, watched the work of his body without interest or participation.

What of the Great Song? Each day Etzwane dutifully went to Kretzel. He played the cantos and memorised the significances, but the project began to loom vast and futile. He could learn the fourteen thousand cantos, and so become another Kretzel . . . Etzwane became wrathful, outraged by his own passivity. 'I defeated the Roguskhoi! I used my energy and intellect! I refused to submit! I must use these same resources to enforce my terms upon destiny!'

So he told himself, and, spiritually regenerated, plotted revolt, sabotage, a guerrilla operation, kidnap and holding of hostages, the capture of the bronze disk-ship beside the compound, signals and communications . . . Each of his schemes foundered on the same reef: impracticality. In frustration he thought to organise a team of kindred spirits, but encountered a discouraging lack of zest. Except in one person, a gaunt and brooding man from the Saprovno district who used the name Shapan, from a weed with tenacious tendrils and fish-hook barbs. Shapan seemed interested in Etzwane's views, and Etzwane began to feel that he had encountered an ally until one day Kretzel casually identified him as the most notorious provocator of the camp. 'He's been the death of a dozen men. He urges them into illicit conduct, then notifies the Ka, and to what purpose other than sheer perversity I cannot fathom, for he has profited not a whit.'

Etzwane became first furious, then disgusted with himself, then sardonically apathetic. Shapan seemed eager to formulate new plots, but Etzwane feigned perplexity.

A clanging of gongs awoke the slaves while darkness still pressed dank and heavy upon the camp. There were flutings and the thud of running feet; emergency of some sort was afoot. From the lumpy cupola atop the garage sounded a wild ululation: the general alarm. The slaves ran forth to find a transport ship at rest in the exercise yard. The slaves stood back, murmuring doubts and speculations.

From the ship came a dozen Ka, asutra clutching their necks. Etzwane sensed haste in their conduct. Ka song-speech, in the 'referential' First Style, fluted across the compound. Again the ululating alarm sounded; the corporals ran forth and ordered their platoons; those who had trained with weapons were marched to the transport ship and up into a long, dim hold. The deck was dirty and layered with filth; the air carried an abominable stench. The slaves stood crowded together, one man's chin on another man's shoulder, and the odor of sweating bodies added a sweet-sour overtone to the reek.

The hulk lurched and moved; the slaves held to stanchions or braced against the hull, or each other; there was no room to fall. Some became sick and commenced a lugubrious groaning; a few began to yell in anger and panic, but were silence by blows. The cries were muffled; the groaning gradually subsided.

An hour, or perhaps two, the ship moved, then jarred to the ground. The engines died; the ship was at rest. With open air so near at hand, the slaves became desperate and began to pound on the hull and to shout, 'Out, out, out . . .'

The hatch opened, admitting a gust of cold wind. The slaves cringed back involuntarily. A voice called, 'Everyone outside, in good order. Danger is at hand; the time has come.'

The slaves hunched out into blowing darkness. A pallid light winked off to the right; a voice called, 'March ahead, towards the light. Stay in line; do not straggle to either side.'

The miserable men stirred; without any particular volition they found themselves trudging along a soft, somewhat spongy surface towards the light. The wind blew steadily, driving a thin, cold rain. Etzwane felt like a man in a terrifying dream, from which he knew he must awake.

The column came to a halt before a low structure. After a wait of a minute or two, it continued forward, down a ramp into an underground hall, dimly illuminated. Drenched and shivering, the slave warriors stood pressed together, vapor rising fetid from their garments. At the far end sounded the fluting of a Ka; the creature mounted a bench, where he was joined by an old man, crooked of body, with extraordinarily long arms and legs.

The Ka produced a set of First Style flutings; the old man spoke, his mouth a black gap at the back of his whiskers. 'I give you the meanings. The enemy has come in a spaceship. They have put down their forts; once again they intend to sweep across Kahei. All the wise helpers they will kill.' He pause to listen to the Ka, and Etzwane wondered who were the 'wise helpers'. Asutra? The old man spoke again. 'The Ka will fight, and you will fight with the Ka, who are your dominants. So you will be joined to the Song.'

The old man listened, but the Ka had no more to say, and the old man spoke alone. 'Look about you now, into each other's faces, because grim events are in the offing and many a man will never see another day. Those who die, how will they be remembered? Not in name nor in semblance, but by their desperate courage. A canto will tell how they went forth in lizard-cars and slid across the dark dawn to measure themselves against the enemy.'

Again the Ka fluted; the old man listened and translated. 'The tactics are simple. In the lizard-cars you are nameless destroyers, the simple essence of desperate rage. Let them fear you! What remains to you except ferocity? When you go, go only forward! The enemy holds the north moor; his forts control the sky. We strike from the ground – '

Etzwane cried out from the dark: 'Who is this "enemy"? They are men like ourselves! Should men kill men in aid of the asutra?'

The old man craned his neck. The Ka fluted; the old man played phrases on his double-pipes, then called to the warriors, 'I know nothing, so ask no questions; I cannot answer. The enemy is the enemy, no matter what his guise. Go forth, destroy! These are the words of the Ka. My own words are these: good luck to all of you. It is an ill business to die so far from Durdane, but die we must, and why not gallantly?'

Another voice, hoarse and mocking, called out, 'Gallantly indeed we will die, and you can assure the Ka of so much; they have not brought us this far for nothing.'

A light flashed red at the end of the chamber. 'Follow the light; step forward then!'

Men milled and circled, none willing to be first. The Ka fluted; the old man cried, 'Out into the passage; go where the red lamp beckons!'

The men surged into a whitewashed tunnel and through a narrow portal at the end; here each man was gripped between two Ka while a third stuck a tube into his mouth and forced a gout of acrid liquid down his throat.

Coughing, cursing, spitting, the men stumbled out upon a pavement and into the watery gray light of the dawn. To either side lizard-cars stood in ranks. The men came slowly forward, and their corporals reached forth and turned them aside, towards a lizard-car. 'In you go,' Polovits told Etzwane in a toneless voice. 'Drive north, over the rise. The torpedo tubes are armed; torpedo the forts, destroy the enemy.'

Etzwane slid into the car; the lid slammed down upon him. He touched the thrust pedal; the car rumbled and hissed and slid off across the pavement and out upon the moor.

Ingenious and dangerous were the lizard-cars: not two feet high, supple and lithe to cling to the contours of the ground. Energy packs were carried in the tail; Etzwane knew nothing of the vehicle's range, but at the training camp they were refueled but seldom. Three torpedo tubes aimed directly forward; the dorsal surface supported a squat, swivel-mounted energy gun. The cars slid on nodes of compression, and in favorable circumstances moved with darting rapidity.

Etzwane drove north up a slope padded with black velvet moss. To either side slid other lizard-cars, some ahead and some behind. The potion which had been forced down his throat now began to take effect: Etzwane felt a grim elation, a sensation of power and invulnerability.

He came up over the roll of the slope and retarded the speed-lever. The control failed to answer. No matter – or so his drugged mind assured him; forward and full speed; what other speed or direction was necessary? . . . He had been tricked. The knowledge eroded his drug-induced élan. He felt sudden prickles of anger. Not enough that they send him forth against 'enemies' he had never known! They also must ensure that he go to his death in haste!

A wide valley spread before him. Two miles away he saw a small, shallow lake, and near by three black spaceships. Lake and spaceships were surrounded by a ring of twenty squat black cones: evidently the forts which the slave warriors had been commanded to attack.

Over the hill came the lizard-cars, one hundred and forty in number, and none could be stopped. One of the cars in front of Etzwane swung about in a great semicircle, and started back the way it had come, the man within waving, gesticulating, pointing. Etzwane and his rancor needed no further stimulus; he turned his own car about and drove back towards the base, yelling in crazy glee out the ventilation ports. One by one the other cars became infected; they veered and darted back the way they had come. On the ridge above crouched four mobile forts, observers within. These forts now slid forward, red lights flashing. Etzwane brought his torpedo sight to bear. He nudged the trigger and one of the forts spun up into the air like a fish breaking water, to crash back down on its side. The other forts opened fire; three lizard-cars became puddles of molten metal, but simultaneously the forts were struck and broken. From two of these clambered Ka, to run across the moor with great striding leaps; after them slid the lizard-cars, harrying, swerving, circling, and finally running down the Ka.

Etzwane waved his arm and bawled out the ventilation ports: 'To the base, to the base!'

Over the hill raced the lizard-cars. Instantly the weapon emplacements beamed glaring red rays of warning. 'Spread apart!' yelled Etzwane. He signaled with his hands, but none heeded. He aimed his torpedo tube and fired; one of the emplacements erupted. The remaining fortifications spat forth lances of energy, burning the lizard-cars at a touch, but other torpedoes struck home. In five seconds half the lizard-cars had become cinders, but the weapons were silenced, and the surviving lizard-cars raced back to the base unopposed. Someone fired a torpedo into the subterranean garage and the entire hill exploded. Turf, concrete, dismembered torsos, miscellaneity spurted high in the air and settled.

The base was a silent crater. The problem now was halting the lizard-cars. Etzwane experimented with the various controls, to no avail. He threw open the entry hatch, to actuate a cut-off switch. The motor died, the car slid to a halt. Etzwane jumped out and stood on the black velvet moss. If he were to be killed in the next minute, he would have died exultant.

The other men halted their cars as Etzwane had done and stepped to the ground. Of the hundred and forty who had set forth, half had returned. The drug still worked its effect; faces were flushed, with eyes prominent and brilliant, and each individual's personality seemed more concentrated, more distinct and powerful than before. They guffawed and stamped and recounted their exploits: ' – outlaws at last, with our lives not worth a twig – ' 'So, then: it's over the hills; into the far places! Let them follow if they dare!' 'Food? Of course there's food! We'll rob the Ka!' ' – vengeance! They won't accept our triumph; they'll drop down from the skies – '

Etzwane spoke: 'A moment; listen to me! Over the hill are the black spaceships. The crews are men like ourselves, from an unknown world. Why should we not go to greet them like friends and trust in their goodwill? We have nothing to lose.'

A brawny, black-bearded man known to Etzwane only as Korba, demanded, 'How do you know there are men aboard these ships?'

'I saw a similar ship broken up,' said Etzwane. 'The bodies of men were expelled. In any event, let us reconnoiter; we have nothing to lose.'

'Correct,' declared Korba. 'We live now from minute to minute.'

'One further matter,' said Etzwane. 'It is important that we act as a group, not a gang of wild men. We need a leader, to coordinate our actions. What of Korba here? Korba, will you undertake to be our leader?'

Korba pulled at his black beard. 'No, not I. You asserted the need and you are the man for the job. What is your name then?'

'I am Gastel Etzwane. I will take the responsibility unless someone objects.'

No one spoke.

'Very well,' said Etzwane. 'First, let us repair the cars, so that we may manage them more easily.'

'Do we need cars?' demanded a hot-eyed old man named Sul, who bore a reputation for disputatiousness. 'Why not move on our own feet and go where the cars cannot go?'

'We may have to range far for food,' said Etzwane. 'We know nothing of the country; the waste may extend a thousand miles. In the cars we have a greater chance of survival, and also the cars are equipped with weapons. We are dangerous warriors in the cars; without them we are a gang of starving fugitives.'

'Correct,' said Korba. 'If the worst occurs, as no doubt it will, we will make them remember us.'

The engine panels were lifted and the clamps removed from the speed controls. Etzwane held up his hand. 'Listen.' Faintly from beyond the hill came a fluctuating wail, of a weird, wild timbre to set the teeth on edge.

The men gave various opinions. 'A signal!' 'No signal; a warning!' 'They know we are here; they are waiting for us.' 'It is a ghost sound, I have heard it near lonesome graves.'

Etzwane said, 'In any case we now set forth. I will lead. At the crest of the hill, we will halt.' He climbed into his car, pulled down the hatch, and set off; the cars slid over the velvet moss like a troop of great black rats.

The hill swelled above them, then flattened, and here the cars halted. The men alighted. Behind them the moor swept down to the crater of the destroyed base and the distant morass; ahead spread the valley, with the pond, the spaceships, and the forts surrounding. About the pond stood a group of twenty men, performing some sort of work. The distance was too great to pick out their features or the nature of their business, but their motions conveyed a sense of urgency. Etzwane became uneasy; the air of the valley was heavy with imminence.

From the spaceships came another wailing call. The men at the pond jerked around, stood rigid a few seconds, then ran back to the ships.

On the hill Korba suddenly called out in awe; he pointed to the south where misty hills loomed up across the dark overcast. Sliding into view from behind these hills came three copper-bronze disk-ships. The first two were of the ordinary sort; the third, an enormous construction, drifted up over the horizon like a copper moon. The first two slid forward with menacing purpose; the large ship drifted more slowly, low to the ground. From the conical forts around the lake came chattering white bolts of light, all striking the leading disk-ship. It gave off a blue coruscation, then bounded high into the sky and was lost to sight in an instant. The second disk-ship stabbed a bar of purple energy at one of the black ships. The forts threw out new energy bolts, but the black ship glowed red, then white, and slumped into an irregular molten mass. The bronze disk then dropped quickly behind a rise of the moor, apparently undamaged. The large disk settled upon the surface near by; its ports snapped open and ramps struck down to the moss. Out surged lizard-cars – twenty, forty, sixty, a hundred. They slid off towards the forts, streaks of black over the black moss, almost invisible and offering no target. The forts moved back towards the globe-ships, but the lizard-cars darted down the black velvet hillside and into torpedo range. The forts discharged bolts of white force; lizard-cars were shattered and flung high into the air. Others discharged torpedoes, and one after another the forts became fragments of torn metal. The lizard-cars hurled torpedoes at the black globe-ships, without effect; the impacts produced only spatters of angry red light. The two bronze disk-ships, the large and the small, lifted into the air and launched thick rods of purple incandescence towards the black globes. Overhead, assistance had arrived. Eight silver-and-white ships of complicated construction, long and slender, dropped down to hang over the black globes. The air flickered and vibrated; the purple bolts became a smoky amber-yellow; they dimmed and died as if the source of their power had failed. The black globes rose into the air and sped off into the sky. They became dark spots on the gray clouds, then plunged through and were gone. The silver-and-white ships hung motionless for three minutes, then plunged away through the clouds.

The lizard-cars slid back to the large disk-ship. They mounted the ramps and disappeared within. Five minutes later, both copper disk-ships rose into the air and departed across the southern hills.

Except for the men on the moor, the panorama was empty of life. Beside the pond remained the exploded forts and the still molten black ship.

The men entered the lizard-cars and gingerly descended the slope to the pond. The forts were tangles of useless metal; the slumped black globe radiated so much heat that no approach could be made. There would be no food taken from this hull. Water however was near at hand. They went down to the edge of the pond. An unpleasant odor arose, which became more intense as they approached. 'Stink or not,' said Korba, 'I will drink; I have forgotten nicety.' He bent to lift up a handful of water, then jerked back. 'The water is full of swimming things.'

Etzwane leaned over the pond. The water swirled with the motion of numberless insect-like creatures, ranging in size from specks to things the length of his hand. From the pinkish-gray torsos grew six small legs, each ending in three tiny fingers. At one end black eye-specks peered from hairy cavities. Etzwane straightened up in disgust. He would drink none of this water. 'Asutra,' he said. 'Asutra by the millions.'

He looked around the sky. Black clouds swept low under the overcast, trailing skeins of rain. Etzwane shivered. 'This is a dire place; the sooner we are gone the better.'

One of the men said dubiously, 'We will be leaving water and food.'

'The asutra?' Etzwane grimaced. 'I'll never be so hungry. In any event they are alien life-stuff and probably poisonous.' He turned away. 'The spaceships may be back; we had better be gone before that time.'

'All very well,' complained old Sul, 'but where is our destination? We are doomed men; why make haste nowhere?'

'I can propose a destination. South beside the morass is the camp, the closest place for food and water.'

The men squinted at him in doubt and puzzlement. Korba demanded somewhat truculently: 'You want us to go back to the camp, when we are free at last?'

Another man grumbled, 'First I'll eat asutra and drink their filth. I was born a Graythorn of the Bagot race, and we are not the sort to enslave ourselves for food.'

'I said nothing of enslaving ourselves,' said Etzwane. 'Have you forgotten the weapons we carry? We do not go to eat slave food; we go to take what we want and to pay off some old debts. We follow the shore south, until we find the camp, then we shall see.'

'It is a far way,' muttered someone.

Etzwane said, 'We came by transport ship in two hours. To return we will ride two days, or three, or four, but there is no help for it.'

'Precisely right,' Korba declared. 'We may be killed by asutra lighting, but none of us expects long life! Let us go seek death on our own terms!'

'Into your cars, then,' said Etzwane. 'We drive south.'

They circled the pond and the smouldering globe-ship, then drove up over the black moor, where rows of glossy tracks indicated the way they had come. Down the long slope they slid, past the exploded base. Somewhere under the rubble, thought Etzwane, lay Polovits, his tyranny completed, his face pressed into the mold. Etzwane felt a grim compassion, in which was mingled outrage for the wrongs done to himself and the human folk. He looked back at the lizard-cars; he and his fellows were as good as dead, but first they would harm their enemies.

The morass was close at hand: a limitless expanse of ooze, blotched with chalk-green scum. The cars swung south and proceeded along the edge of the moor. Clouds hung heavy and low; in the distance moor, morass and sky blurred together without discernible line of conjunction.

South slid the cars, a supple, sinister train, the men never looking back. During the afternoon they came to a slough of brackish dark water, of which they drank, despite a bitter aftertaste, and filled the receptacles within the cars; then, fording the slough at the very brink of the morass, they continued south.

The sky darkened; the evening rain fell, to be instantly absorbed by the moss. The cars proceeded through the dusk, which presently became darkness. Etzwane brought the column to a halt and the men climbed out upon the moss, groaning for their sore muscles and hunger. They stretched and hobbled back and forth along the line, muttering in gruff, hoarse voices. Some, noting how distinct was the division between the luminous ooze of the morass and the dead blackness of the moor, wanted to drive on through the night. 'The sooner we come to the camp the sooner we make an end to the matter; we will eat or be killed.'

'I am also in haste,' said Etzwane, 'but the dark is too dangerous. We have no lights and cannot stay together. What if someone becomes torpid and goes to sleep? Hungry or not, we must wait for day.'

'In the light we are visible to skycraft,' argued one of the men. 'There are dangers in both directions, but our bellies howl for food regardless.'

'We'll start as soon as the dawn gives light,' said Etzwane. 'To travel through the black night is folly. My belly is as slack as anyone's; for lack of anything better I plan to sleep.' He troubled to talk no further, and went down to the shore to look out over the morass. The ooze glowed blue in lines and reticulations, these slowly moving and forming new patterns. Flickers of pale light hung in the reeds and moved in wisps across the open spaces . . . At Etzwane's feet something scuttled across the mud; by its outline he saw it to be a large, flat insect, walking on a dozen pads across the ooze. He peered close. An asutra? No, something different, but perhaps in just some similar swamp had the asutra evolved. Perhaps even on Kahei, though the first cantos of the Great Song made no reference to asutra . . . Others of the group walked by the shore, marveling at the lights and the eerie solitude . . . Along the shore someone struck a tiny fire, using dried bits of moss and reed for fuel. Etzwane saw that several men had captured insects and were preparing to toast and eat them. Etzwane gave a fatalistic shrug. He was leader by the most tenuous of contracts.

The night was long in passing. Etzwane tried to find room to sleep within the lizard-car, then came forth and lay down upon the moss. A cold wind blew through the night, allowing him no real comfort. He dozed . . . Sounds of anguish awakened him. He rose to his feet and felt his way along the line of cars. Three men lay on the ground, retching convulsively. Etzwane stood a moment, then went back to his car. He could offer neither comfort nor help; indeed so close about them hung doom that the death of three men seemed of no great import . . . A misty rain slanted down on the wind. Etzwane once more entered the car. The groans of the poisoned men became less distinct, and presently were heard no more.

Dawn finally arrived, and three men lay dead upon the

spongy black turf: the three who had eaten insects. Without comment Etzwane went to his car, and the column proceeded south.

The moors seemed endless; the men drove the cars in a semitorpor. At noon they came upon another slough, and drank of the water. The reeds surrounding carried clusters of waxy fruit, which one or two of the men gingerly examined. Etzwane said nothing, and the men turned reluctantly away.

Korba stood looking along the moors to the south. He pointed to a far shadow which might be either a cloud or a jutting mountain. 'North of the camp rose a crag,' said Korba, 'perhaps that which lies ahead.'

'We have farther to go,' said Etzwane. 'The ship which took us north moved at a considerable speed. I suspect that two days of travel, or more, still lie ahead.'

'If our bellies will give us the strength.'

'Our bellies will take us there if the cars will do so. This is my main fear, that the cars will exhaust their energy.'

Korba and the others looked askance at the long black shapes. 'Let us move on,' said one of the men. 'At least we shall see the other side of the hills, and by luck Korba may have the accurate prediction.'

'I hope so too,' said Etzwane. 'Still, be prepared for disappointment.'

The column proceeded across an undulating black carpet of moss. Nowhere was there evidence of life; no motion, no ruined dwelling, no ancient post or cairn.

A brief storm struck down upon them; black clouds boiled low; a sudden wind came roaring out of the west . . . In half an hour the storm had passed, leaving the air clearer than before. The shadow to the south was clearly a mountain of considerable mass.

Close upon the end of day the column breasted the ridge to look out over the panorama. As far as the eye could reach appeared empty black moor.

The column halted: the men came forth from the cars to stare over the desolation ahead. Etzwane said briefly, 'We have far to go.' He reentered his car and slid away downhill.

A project had formed in his mind, and when darkness forced a halt he explained his plan. 'Remember the disk-ship which waits at the camp? I believe it to be a space vessel; in any case it is an object of great value, worth far more than the deaths of fifty or sixty men. If a ship is in fact still at the camp, I suggest that we capture it, and bargain our way back to Durdane.'

'Can we do this?' asked Korba. 'Will they not detect us and use their torpedoes?'

'I noticed no great vigilance at the camp,' said Etzwane. 'Why should we not attempt the maximum? For a certainty no one will help us but ourselves.'

One of the Alula said in a bitter voice, 'I had forgotten; so many events have come and gone. Long ago you told us of the planet Earth and mentioned a certain Ifness.'

'A fantasy,' said Etzwane. 'I too have forgotten . . . Strange to think! For the folk of Earth, did they know of us, we would be creatures of a nightmare, less than wisps of the swamp-light yonder . . . I fear that I will never see Earth.'

'I would be happy to see old Caraz,' said the Alula. 'I would think myself fortunate beyond belief and never grieve again.'

One of the men growled, 'I would be content for a chunk of fat meat.'

One at a time, reluctant to leave the warmth of companionship, the men went off to their cars and passed another dreary night.

As soon as dawn made the land distinct, they were under way. Etzwane's car seemed not as lively as before;

he wondered how many miles remained in its engine. How far ahead lay the camp? One day at least, three or four days at most.

The moss stretched ahead flat and soggy, almost one with the quagmire. Several times the cars passed pools of gray mud. Near one of these the column halted to rest and ease cramped muscles. The pools quaked with huge miasmic bubbles, rising with an unctuous suck. The periphery of the mud was home to colonies of jointed brown worms and running black balls, both of which submerged themselves in the mud at a sound: a fact which puzzled Etzwane; there seemed no natural enemy from which the creatures would be required to protect themselves. Etzwane searched the air: no birds, flying reptiles, nor winged insects. In the fringe of rotten black moss three or four feet back from the shore of mud he spied small burrows, from which issued the prints of small, three-fingered members. Etzwane examined the prints with frowning suspicion In the moss a small purplish-black shape moved back into concealment: an asutra, not yet mature. Etzwane drew back, alarmed and repelled. When races derived from such disparate environments as man and asutra, could there possibly be communication or sympathy? Etzwane thought not. A tolerance founded on mutual distaste, possibly; cooperation, never.

The column proceeded, and now one of the cars began to falter, rising and falling on its support nodes. The car at last sank down upon the moor and would go no further. Etzwane put the driver astride the most fresh-seeming car; once again the column proceeded.

During the middle afternoon two other cars subsided upon the moss; it was plain that a very few hours remained to any of the engines. Ahead rose another black hill, which seemed lower than that hill north of camp. If it were another hill, Etzwane thought they would never see the camp, for none of the men had the strength to walk thirty or forty or fifty miles.

They swung out close to the morass to avoid the heights; even so the mountain met the morass in a precipitous bluff, over which they laboriously climbed.

Up towards the ridge moved the lizard-cars, groaning and sagging. Etzwane led the way over the crest, the landscape to the south opened before them . . . The camp lay below, not five miles distant. A husky roar rose from fifty dry throats. 'The camp; down to the camp! Food awaits us; bread, good soup!'

Etzwane tottered out of his car. 'Hold back, you fools! Have you forgotten our plan?'

'Why should we wait?' croaked Sul. 'Look! There is no spaceship on the premises; it is gone! Even if there were, your scheme is absurd. We shall eat and drink; all else is now meaningless. On then, down to the camp!'

Etzwane said, 'Hold back! We have suffered too much to throw away our lives now. There is no spaceship, true! But we must make ourselves masters of the camp, and this means surprise. We will wait for dusk. You must control your appetite until then.'

'I have not come all this distance to suffer further,' declared Sul.

'Suffer or die,' growled Korba. 'When the camp is ours, then you shall eat. Now is the time to prove ourselves men, not slaves!'

Sul said no more. Ashen-faced he leaned back against his car, mumbling through dry gray lips.

The camp seemed curiously listless and desolate. A few women moved about their duties; a Ka came briefly forth from the far barracks. It walked aimlessly back and forth, then reentered. No squads drilled upon the compound; the garage was dark.

Korba whispered, 'The camp is dead; there is no one to stop us.'

'I am suspicious,' said Etzwane. 'The quiet is unnatural.'

'You believe that they expect us?'

'I don't know what to believe. We still must wait till dusk, even if the camp is empty except for three Ka and a dozen old women, so that they can't send off a message of emergency.'

Korba grunted.

'The sky is darkening already,' said Etzwane. 'In another hour the dusk will hide our approach.'

The group waited, pointing here and there at remembered corners of the camp. Lamps began to glow, and Etzwane looked at Korba. 'Are you ready?'

'I am ready.'

'Remember, I will attack the Ka barracks from the side; you enter the camp from the front and destroy whatever resistance appears.'

'The plan is clear.'

Etzwane and half the cars descended the flank of the hill, dark cars invisible on the black moss. Korba waited five minutes, then proceeded down the slope, approaching the camp across the old training compound. Etzwane's group, with cars dragging and bumping across the moss, drove up to the back of the lumpy white structure which the Ka used as a barracks.

The men lunged inside and swarmed upon the seven Ka they found in the single chamber. Astonished or perhaps apathetic, the Ka made only feeble resistance and were lashed immobile with thongs. The men, keyed up for a desperate battle and finding none, felt baffled and frustrated, and started to kick the Ka to death. Etzwane halted them in a fury. 'What are you doing? They are victims like ourselves. Kill the asutra, but do no harm to the Ka! It is purposeless!'

The men thereupon plucked the asutra off the Ka's necks and ground them underfoot, to the horrified moaning of the Ka.

Etzwane went forth to find Korba, who had already sent his men into the garages, the commissary, and the communication chamber, where they had discovered a total of four Ka, three of which they clubbed to pulp, lacking Etzwane's moderating presence. The men encountered no other opposition; they were masters of the camp, almost without effort. Reacting to the tension, many of the men became nauseated. Sagging to their knees they gave themselves to an agonised, empty-stomached retching. Etzwane, himself hearing strange ringing sounds in his ears, ordered the women of the camp instantly to serve hot food and drink.

The men ate, slowly, gratefully, marveling that the storming of the camp had gone with such facility. The situation was incredible.

After eating, Etzwane felt an overpowering drowsiness, to which he must not allow himself to succumb. Old Kretzel stood near by, and he called for her. 'What has happened to the Ka? There were forty or fifty in the camp; now there are ten or less.'

Kretzel spoke in a dismal voice. 'They departed in the ship. Only two days ago they went, in great excitement. Great events are in the offing, for better or worse.'

'When will another ship return?'

'They did not trouble to explain this to me.'

'Let us question the Ka.'

They went to the barracks where the Ka lay bound. The ten men Etzwane had left on guard were all asleep and the Ka were furiously working to liberate themselves. Etzwane roused the sleeping men with kicks. 'Is this the way you guard our safety? Every one of you: dead to the world! In another minute you might have been dead forever.'

Old Sul, one of the men who had been left on guard, gave a surly response, 'You yourself described these men as victims; in all justice they should be grateful for their deliverance.'

'This is precisely the point I intend to make to them,' said Etzwane. 'Meanwhile we are only the wild men who attacked them and tied them with thongs.'

'Bah,' muttered Sul. 'I am unable to chop logic with you; you have the superior sleight with words.'

Etzwane said, 'Make sure the thongs are secure.' He spoke to Kretzel. 'Tell the Ka that we mean them no harm, that we regard the asutra as our mutual enemy.'

Kretzel peered at Etzwane in perplexity, as if she found the remarks strange and foolish. 'Why do you tell them that?'

'So that they will help us, or at least do nothing to hinder.'

She shook her head. 'I'll sing to them, but they will pay no great heed. You do not understand the Ka.' She took up her double-pipes and played phrases. The Ka listened without perceptible reaction. They made no reply, but after a brief silence made wavering, tremulous sounds, like the chuckling of baby owls.

Etzwane looked at them doubtfully. 'What do they say?'

Kretzel shrugged. 'They talk together in the "Allusivc" Style, which is beyond my capability. In any event, I don't think they understand you.'

'Ask them when the ship will return.'

Kretzel laughed but obliged him. The Ka looked at her blankly. One warbled a brief phrase, then they were silent. Etzwane looked questioningly at Kretzel.

'They sing from Canto 5633: the "embarrassing farce". It might translate as a jeer: "What interest can this matter have for you?" '

'I see,' said Etzwane. 'They are not practical.'

'They are practical enough,' said Kretzel. 'The situation is beyond their understanding. Do you remember the ahulphs of Durdane?'

'I do indeed.'

'To the Ka, men are like ahulphs: unpredictable, half-intelligent, addicted to incomprehensible antics. They cannot take you seriously.'

Etzwane grunted. 'Ask the question again. Tell them that when the ship arrives they will be freed.'

Kretzel played her flute. A terse answer returned. 'The ship will be back in a few days with a new corps of slaves.'

Chapter 10

The mutinous slaves had gained themselves food, shelter, and a respite which all realised to be temporary. A certain Joro argued that the group should transport supplies to some secret place in the hills and hope to survive until they could dare another raid. 'By this means we gain another several months, and who knows what might happen? The rescue ships from Earth might arrive.'

Etzwane gave a bitter laugh. 'I know now what I should have known every moment of my life; that unless you help yourself, you die a slave. The fact is basic. No one is going to rescue us. If we remain here, the chances are good that we will shortly be killed. If we go out to hide upon the moors, we gain two months of wet clothes and misery, and then we will be killed anyway. If we pursue the original plan, at best we gain a great advantage and at worst we die in dignity, doing our enemies as much damage as possible.'

'The chances of "best" are few and of "worst" many,' grumbled Sul. 'I for one am fatigued with these visionary schemes.'

'You must do as you think best,' said Etzwane politely. 'By all means, go forth upon the moors. The way is open.'

Korba said curtly, 'Those who want to go, let them go now. The rest of us have work to do, and time may be short.'

But neither Sul nor Joro chose to leave.

During the day Rune the Willow Wand approached Etzwane. 'Do you remember me? I am the Alul girl who once befriended you. I wonder if you think warmly of me now? But I am haggard and wrinkled, as if I were old. Is this not true?'

Etzwane, preoccupied with a hundred anxieties, looked across the compound, trying to contrive a remark suitably noncommittal. He said, somewhat curtly, 'On this world a pretty girl is a freak.'

'Ah! I wish then I were a freak! So long ago, when the men reached to tweak off my little cap, I was happy, even though I pretended displeasure. But now, if I were to dance naked in the compound, who would look at me?'

'You would still attract attention,' said Etzwane. 'Especially if you danced well.'

'You mock me,' said Rune sorrowfully. 'Why cannot you offer me some consolation: a touch or a smiling glance? You make me feel squat and ugly.'

'I have no such intention,' said Etzwane. 'You may be assured of this. But please excuse me; I must see to our preparations.'

Two days went past, with tension increasing every hour. On the morning of the third day a disk-ship slid up the coast from the south and hovered over the camp. There was no need for alarms or exhortations; the men were already at their stations.

The ship hovered, hanging on a humming web of vibration. Etzwane, in the garage, watched with clammy sweat on his body, wondering which of many circumstances would go wrong.

From the ship came a mellow hooting, which after an interval reverberated back from the hill.

The sound died, the ship hovered. Etzwane held his breath until his lungs ached.

The ship moved, and slowly descended to the landing field. Etzwane exhaled and leaned forward. This now was the time of crisis.

The ship touched the ground, which visibly subsided under the mass of the ship. A minute passed, two minutes. Etzwane wondered if those aboard had perceived an incorrectness, the absence of some formality . . . The port opened; a ramp slid to the soil. Down came two Ka, asutra riding their necks like small black jockeys. They halted at the base of the ramp, looked across the compound. Two more Ka descended the ramp, and the four stood as if waiting.

A pair of drays set out from the warehouse: the usual procedure when a ship landed. They swerved to pass close to the ramp. Etzwane and three men came forth from the garage, to walk with simulated purposelessness towards the ship. From other areas of the yard other small groups of men converged upon the ship.

The first dray halted; four men stepped down and suddenly leapt upon the Ka. From the second dray four other men brought thongs; there would be only needful killing, lest they be left with a ship and no one to navigate. While the group struggled at the foot of the ramp, Etzwane and his men ran up the ramp and into the ship.

The ship carried a crew of fourteen Ka and several dozens of asutra, some in trays like that which Etzwane and Ifness had found in the wreck under Thrie Orgai. Except for the scuffle at the foot of the ramp, neither Ka nor asutra offered resistance. The Ka had seemed paralysed by surprise, or perhaps apathetic; there was no comprehending their emotions. The asutra were as opaque as flint. Again the rebel slaves felt the frustration of over-exertion, of striking out with all force and encountering only air. They felt relieved but cheated, triumphant yet seething with unrelieved tension.

The great central hold contained almost four hundred men and women. These were of all ages and conditions, but in general seemed of poor quality, spiritless and defeated.

Etzwane wasted no time upon the folk in the hold; he gathered the Ka and their asutra in the control dome and brought up Kretzel. 'Tell them this,' said Etzwane, 'and make sure that they comprehend exactly. We want to return to Durdane. This is what we require of them: transportation to our home-world. We will tolerate nothing less. Tell them that when we arrive at our destination, then we will make no further demands upon them; they may have their lives and their ship. If they refuse to take us to Durdane, we will destroy them without mercy.'

Kretzel frowned and licked her lips, then brought forth her pipes and played Etzwane's message.

The Ka stood unresponsive. Etzwane asked anxiously, 'Do they understand?'

'They understand,' said Kretzel. 'They have already decided what their answer will be. This is a ceremonial silence.'

One of the Ka addressed Kretzel in a set of careful First Style tones, delivered in a manner so offhand as to seem condescending or even derisive.

Kretzel said to Etzwane, 'They will take you to Durdane. The ship departs at once.'

'Ask if sufficient food and drink are aboard.'

Kretzel obeyed and elicited a reply. 'He says that provisions are naturally adequate for the journey.'

'Tell them one thing further. We have brought torpedoes aboard the ship. If they try to deceive us, we will all blow up together.'

Kretzel played her double-pipes; the Ka turned away without interest.

Etzwane had known many triumphs and joys during the course of his life, but never exhilaration such as now, on this journey back from the dark world Kahei. He felt tired but he could not sleep. He distrusted the Ka, he feared the asutra; he could not believe that his victory was final. Of the other men he felt confidence only in Korba, and he made certain that he and Korba never slept at the same time. To maintain a spirit of vigilance, he warned that the asutra were devious, that they did not readily accept defeat; privately he was sure that victory had been won. In his experience the asutra were impassive realists, unaffected by considerations of malice or revenge. When the Roguskhoi had been defeated in Shant, the asutra might easily have destroyed Garwiy and Brassei and Maschein with their energy bolts, but had not troubled to do so. Chances were good, thought Etzwane, that the impossible had been accomplished, and without the assistance of the ineffable Ifness, which added savor to the triumph.

Etzwane spent considerable time in the control dome. Through the ports nothing could be seen but dead blackness and an occasional streaming filament of spume. A panel depicted the outside sky; the stars were black disks on a luminous green field. A target circle enclosed three black dots, which daily grew larger; Etzwane assumed these to be Etta, Sassetta, and Zael.

Conditions in the hold were appalling. The cargo of men and women were ignorant of cleanliness, order, or sanitation; the hold stank like an abattoir. Etzwane learned that most of the folk had been born on Kahei and had known only the life of the slave camp. During the evolution of the Roguskhoi, macabre experiments had been part of their everyday routine; it had seemed the natural way of life. The asutra, whatever their virtues, displayed neither squeamishness nor pity, thought Etzwane, and perhaps these were emotions idiosyncratically human. Etzwane tried to feel compassion for the slave folk, but the stench and disorder in the hold made the task difficult. Once more on Durdane, these folk were destined for further misery. Some might wish themselves 'back home' on the black world Kahei.

The ship coasted through open space. Above danced the three suns; below spread the gray-violet face of Durdane. As the ship descended, familiar contours passed below: the Beljamar and the Fortunate Isles, Shant and Palasedra, then the vast world-continent Caraz.

Etzwane identified the river Keba and Lake Nior. As the ship dropped lower, the Thrie Orgai and the river Vurush appeared. With Kretzel's assistance he directed the ship down to Shagfe. The ship landed on the slope south of the village. The ramps descended; the passengers tumbled, staggered, and crawled out upon the soil of their home-world, each clutching a parcel of food and as much good metal as he could carry: enough to assure a comfortable competence on metal-poor Durdane. Etzwane provided himself with thirty rods of glistening red alloy from the engine room: enough wealth, so he calculated, to bring him once again to Shant.

Ever distrustful, Etzwane insisted that the Ka come forth from the ship and remain until the folk had dispersed. 'You have brought us here to Durdane, and now we are finished with you and your ship, but are you finished with us? I don't want to be destroyed by a purple lightning bolt that you discharge as soon as you have the capability.'

Through Kretzel the Ka responded, 'We don't care whether you live or die; leave the ship at once.'

Etzwane said, 'Either come out on the plain with us or we will remove your asutra, which you seem to revere so much. We have not suffered and hoped and striven to take foolish chances at the last moment.'

Eight of the Ka at last went out on the plain. Etzwane, with a group of his men, led them a mile up the slope, then dismissed them. They trudged back to their ship while Etzwane and his companions sought shelter among the rocks. As soon as the eight were aboard, the ship lifted into the air. Etzwane watched it dwindle and vanish, then within himself the knowledge came: he had really returned to Durdane. His knees felt limp; he sat down upon a rock, weary as he had never been before in his life, and tears flowed from his eyes.

Chapter 11

In Shagfe the advent of so many persons laden with wealth had created dislocations. Some drank copiously of Baba's cellar brew, others gambled with the Kash Blue-worms, who still haunted the vicinity. Throughout the night sounds of altercation could be heard: yells and curses, drunken sobs and cries of pain; and in the morning a dozen corpses were discovered. As soon as light came to the sky, groups set forth for their ancestral lands, to north, east, south, and west. The Alula, uttering no words of farewell to Etzwane, departed for Lake Nior. Rune the Willow Wand turned a single glance over her shoulder. Etzwane, meeting the gaze, found it unreadable. He watched them recede into the morning haze, then he went to find Baba the innkeeper.

'I have two matters to take up with you,' said Etzwane. 'First, where is Fabrache?'

Baba replied in vague terms. 'Who is to trace the course of that loose-footed man? The slave trade is ruined. Old markets are gone and Hozman Sore-throat has disappeared; poverty stalks the land. As for Fabrache, when he appears you will see him; he is not a man for predictability.'

'I will not wait,' said Etzwane, 'which leads me to the second matter, my pacer. I desire that it be saddled and made ready for travel.'

Baba's eyes protruded in wonder. 'Your pacer? What prodigy of imagination is this? You own no pacer at my stables.'

'But indeed I do,' said Etzwane in a sharp voice. 'My friend Ifness and I both left our pacers in your care. I, at least, now intend to resume possession.'

Baba shook his head in wonder and raised his eyes piously to the sky. 'In your own land odd customs may prevail, but here at Shagfe we are more practical. A gift once given may not be recalled.'

'Gift, you say?' Etzwane's tone was grim. 'Have you heard the tales told by the folk who brought you metal for cellar brew last night? How by our strength and will we won our way home to Caraz? Do you think that I am the kind of man to tolerate petty thievery? Bring me my pacer, or prepare for a remarkable thrashing.'

Baba reached behind his bar and brought forth his cudgel. 'A beating, is it? Listen to me, my cockscomb, I have not been Shagfe innkeeper without dealing a few beatings of my own, I assure you. Now leave these premises on the instant!'

From his pouch Etzwane brought the little weapon Ifness had given him so long ago: the energy gun he had carried to Kahei and back and never used. He pointed the gun at Baba's strongbox and touched the button. A flare, an explosion, a scream of horror, as Baba stared at the devastation which only a moment before had held a fortune in metal. Etzwane reached out, took his cudgel, and hit him across the back. 'My pacer, and in haste.'

Baba's fat face was lambent with fear and malice. 'Already you have done me out of a lifetime's earnings! Do you wish the fruits of all my toil?'

'Never try to cheat an honest man,' said Etzwane. 'Another thief might sympathise with your goals; as for me, I want only my property.'

In a voice nasal with rage Baba sent one of the yard-boys to the stables. Etzwane went out into the inn-yard, where he found old Kretzel sitting on a bench. 'What do you do here?' asked Etzwane. 'I thought that you would be on your way to Elshuka Pond.'

'The way is long,' said Kretzel, pulling the tattered cloak about her shoulders. 'I have a few bits of metal, enough to keep food in my mouth for a period. When the metal is gone I shall start my journey south, though surely I will never arrive at the grass meadows above the pond. And if I did, who would remember the little girl who was stolen by Molsk?'

'What of the Great Song? How many people of Shagfe will understand when you play your pipes?'

Kretzel huddled her old shoulders into the sunlight's warmth. 'It is a great epic: the history of a far world. Perhaps I will forget, but perhaps not, and sometimes when I sit here in the sun I will play the pipes, but no one will know the great deeds I relate.'

The pacer was led forth: a creature by no means as sound as that Etzwane had brought to Shagfe, with gear somewhat worn and makeshift. Etzwane pointed out these facts, and the boy brought him out sacks of meal and a bladder of cellar brew for the journey.

Standing by the side of the inn Etzwane saw a familiar face: it belonged to Gulshe, who watched his preparations with a lowering intensity. Gulshe would make an efficient guide, reflected Etzwane, but what of the times when Etzwane slept and Gulshe kept watch? The prospect caused Etzwane to shudder. He gave Gulshe a polite salute and mounted his pacer. For a moment he looked down upon old Kretzel, her head stored with wonderful knowledge. He never would see her again, and with her would die the history of a world . . . Kretzel looked up; their gazes met. Etzwane turned away, his eyes again full of tears. He departed Shagfe, and against his back he felt Gulshe's stare and Kretzel's farewell.

Four days later Etzwane rode over a jutting sandstone crest and looked down on the flowing Keba. Shillinsk, by his rough reckoning, should lie somewhat south, for he had lost his way crossing the Plain of Blue Flowers. He looked up the Keba shore and five miles south spied the Shillinsk dock. He turned the pacer down the slope and rode south.

The Shillinsk Inn was as he had remembered it. Neither cargo vessel nor barge was moored alongside the dock, but Etzwane felt no great impatience; the tranquility of Shillinsk was a thing to be enjoyed in itself.

He entered the inn to find the landlord polishing the surface of his counter with a bag of rottenstone and a greasy square of chumpa-skin. He failed to recognise Etzwane, for which Etzwane felt no surprise. In his ragged garments he was a far remove from that spruce Gastel Etzwane who had come to Shillinsk with Ifness.

'You will not remember me,' said Etzwane, 'but some months ago I came here with the sorcerer Ifness in his magic boat. You were the victim of an unpleasant incident, as I recall.'

The landlord grimaced. 'Do not bring such matters to my attention. The sorcerer Ifness is a man to be feared. When will he come for his boat? It floats yonder on the water.'

Etzwane stared in surprise. 'Ifness has not taken his boat?'

'Look through the doorway; you will see it, exactly as you left it.' And he added virtuously, 'I have kept the craft secure and unmolested, as I was charged.'

'Well done.' Etzwane was greatly pleased; he had watched Ifness at the controls; he knew the use of the dials and also knew how to board the boat without suffering an electric shock. He indicated the pacer. 'For your trouble I hereby make you the gift of yonder pacer, with his saddle. I require only a meal and lodging for the night; tomorrow I sail away in the magic boat.'

'You will take it to Ifness?'

'In all truth, I can't imagine what has happened to him. I expected that he would have come to Shillinsk long ago and taken the boat himself . . . No doubt, if he requires either me or the boat, he will know where to find me – if he is still alive.'

If Ifness were still alive. Between Shagfe and Shillinsk lay a hundred dangers: chumpa, bands of crazy ahulph, robber tribes, and slavers. Ifness might have fallen victim to any of these, and all of Etzwane's hard thoughts might be unjustified . . . Should he go forth to seek Ifness? Etzwane heaved a long sigh. Caraz was vast. It would be an exercise in futility.

The landlord prepared a savory supper of river fish poached in a tart green sauce, and Etzwane walked out on the dock to watch purple dusk fall over the water. Shant and the city Garwiy were much closer than he had hoped.

In the morning he rowed out to the boat in a skiff and gingerly prodded the guard-switch with a dry stick. Then even more gingerly he laid his finger on the gunwale. No shock, no coruscation of sparks like that which had flung the landlord into the river.

Etzwane tied the skiff to the mooring line and cast off. The current caught the boat and carried it north and out into the stream. He hoisted the sail; Shillinsk receded, and became a line of toy houses on the shore.

Now: the critical experiment. He opened the console and examined the line of knobs. Cautiously he twisted the 'Ascensor'. Up rose the boat, gliding on the wind. Etzwane hurriedly lowered the sail lest a gust capsize him.

He tested the other knobs; the boat swung in a wide arc and flew east towards Shant.

Below passed the dove-gray plains and dark-green swamps. Ahead glistened the Bobol River, and then the great Usak.

By night Etzwane reached the east coast and the Green Ocean. A few flickering yellow lights indicated a shore-side village; ahead the stars reflected on the water.

Etzwane slowed the boat, so that it drifted, and slept; and when dawn came, the land of Shant loomed along the horizon to the southeast.

Etzwane flew high above cantons Gitanesq and Fenesq, then descended towards the Sualle. The towers of Garwiy could barely be seen: a handful of glowing jewels. The shores closed in; fishing boats worked in the distance. Etzwane dropped the boat into the water. He hoisted the sail, and with the wind at his back, drove with a bubbling wake towards Garwiy.

The wind presently slackened and the boat moved more slowly over the placid water. Drowsing in the warmth, Etzwane could find no occasion for haste; indeed, the prospect of docking the boat and stepping ashore aroused in him a curious mood of melancholy. The adventure would then be definitely finished; for all its misery and black despair, he had lived to his utmost capacity; he had augmented and enriched his life.

Across the halcyon water sailed the boat, and the towers of Garwiy reared above him like lords at a banquet. Along the shore Etzwane spied familiar sights: this building, that warehouse, and there the ramshackle old dock at which Ifness had moored his boat. Etzwane swung the tiller, the boat gurgled through the water. Etzwane dropped the sail; the boat coasted quietly to the pier.

Etzwane made the boat secure, then walked up into the

road and hailed a diligence. The driver looked him over with misgivings. 'Well, then, why do you stop me? I have nothing to give; go to the public hospital for your alms.'

'I want no alms; I want transportation,' said Etzwane. He climbed into the diligence. 'Take me to Fontenay's Inn, on Galias Avenue.'

'You have money?'

'Not in these garments. At Fontenay's you will be paid; accept my word for this.'

The driver flicked the pacer into motion. Etzwane called up to him, 'What has been happening in Garwiy? I have been away for months.'

'Nothing of any great moment. The Green and Purple have weighed us down with taxes; they are more ambitious with their schemes than was the Anome . . . I like air at my neck instead of the torc, but now the Green and Purple want me to pay for my liberty. Which is better: cheap submission or expensive independence?'

Through the dusk rolled the diligence, along streets which seemed quaint and small, dearly familiar and somehow remote. On Kahei, Garwiy had seemed a dream – yet it existed. Here in Garwiy, Kahei had become an abstraction – and it too existed. Elsewhere was the world of the black globe-ships with the human crews. He would never learn the actuality of this world.

The diligence halted before Fontenay's Inn; the driver looked truculently down at Etzwane. 'Now then, my money, if you please.'

'One moment.' Etzwane went into the inn, to find Fontenay sitting at a table enjoying a flask of his own merchandise. Fontenay frowned at the ragged apparition, then recognising Etzwane, uttered an ejaculation of astonishment. 'What is this? Gastel Etzwane in rags for a charade?'

'No charade, but an adventure from which I have only

now returned. Be so good as to pay off this importunate driver, then let me have a room, a bath, a barber, some fresh garments, and finally a good dinner.'

'Nothing could give me more pleasure,' said Fontenay. He snapped his fingers. 'Heinel! Jared! See to Gastel Etzwane's convenience!' Fontenay turned back to Etzwane. 'Can you guess who plays music on yonder bandstand? In half an hour he will arrive.'

'Dystar the druithine?'

'Alas, not Dystar! It is Frolitz and his Pink-Black-Azure-Deep Greeners.'

'This is good news,' said Etzwane from the depths of his heart. 'I can think of no one I would rather see.'

'Well then, make yourself comfortable. A merry evening lies before us.'

Etzwane bathed himself with zeal: the first warm bath he had known since departing Fontenay's with Ifness. He dressed in fresh garments, then a barber trimmed his hair and shaved his face. What of his sour-smelling rags? He was tempted to keep them for mementos, but threw them away.

He went down to the common room, to find Frolitz in conversation with Fontenay. Frolitz leapt to his feet and embraced Etzwane. 'Well then, my lad! I haven't seen you for months, and I hear that you have enjoyed a picaresque adventure! You always were the one for foibles and quixotries! But now, here you are, and looking – how shall I say it? – full of strange knowledge. What music have you been playing?'

Etzwane laughed. 'I started to learn a Great Song of fourteen thousand cantos, but mastered only twenty or thereabouts.'

'A good beginning! Perhaps we shall hear some of these tonight. I have taken on another man, a clever young Paganese, but he lacks elasticity. I doubt if he will ever learn. You shall have your old seat and Chaddo can work the sliding bass. What do you say to that?'

'I say, first, that I cannot play tonight; I would astound you all! Second, I am famished for a meal; I have been to Caraz and subsisted on porridge. Third, in regard to the future; it is a void.'

'Outside interests constantly interfere with your music,' declared Frolitz peevishly. 'I suppose you came to meet your old friend, whose name I forget. I have seen him often during the past few days; for a fact, there he goes now, to his usual table in the corner. Take my advice and ignore him.'

'The advice is good,' said Etzwane in a strained voice. 'Nevertheless, I must have a word with Ifness, and I will join you later.'

Etzwane crossed the room, to stand before the table in the corner. 'I am surprised to see you.'

Ifness looked up blankly then gave a brusque nod. 'Ah, Etzwane, you catch me at a hurried moment. I must take a quick meal and depart.'

Etzwane sank into a chair and stared into the long, austere face as if to bring forth Ifness' secrets by visual suction. 'Ifness, one of us must be insane. Who is it, you or I?'

Ifness made an irritated gesture. 'It would work to the same effect; in either case an equal disparity of opinion would exist. But, as I put forward, I –'

Etzwane spoke as if he had not heard. 'Do you recall the circumstances of our leave-taking?'

Ifness frowned. 'Why should I not do so? The event occurred at a place in north-central Caraz on a day I cannot precisely name. I believe that you departed in pursuit of a barbarian maiden, or some such thing. As I recall, I warned you against the project.'

'This was the general nature of the event. You went off to arrange a rescue operation.'

A waiter set a tureen before Ifness, who raised the lid, sniffed, then ladled forth a bowl of green sea-fruit soup. Ifness came back to Etzwane's remark with an abstracted frown. 'Let me see; what were the circumstances? They included the Alul tribesmen and Hozman Sore-throat. You wanted to organise a gallant expedition into the skies to rescue a girl who had struck your fancy. I pronounced such an effort impractical and even suicidal. I am glad to see that you were dissuaded.'

'I remember the matter from a different perspective,' said Etzwane. 'I proposed to capture the depot ship; you stated that such an acquisition would interest the Earth folk and that a rescue ship might arrive in a minimum of two or three weeks.'

'Yes, this was the case. I mentioned the matter to Dasconetta, who felt that such a step exceeded the capabilities of his office, and nothing came of it.' Ifness tasted of his soup and sprinkled a few flakes of pepper pod upon the surface. 'In any case, the eventualities were the same, and you need feel no more concern.'

Etzwane controlled his voice with an effort. 'How could eventualities be the same when a shipload of captives is taken to a far planet?'

'I speak in a broad sense,' said Ifness. 'As for myself, my work has taken me far afield.' He glanced at his chronometer. 'I have yet a few minutes. The asutra that I took here in Shant, and others, have been studied. You may be interested in what I have learned.'

Etzwane leaned back in his chair. 'By all means, tell me about the asutra.'

Ifness consumed his soup with slow, easy sweeps of the spoon. 'Something of what I will tell you is conjecture, some is induction, some observations, and some derives from direct communication. The asutra are a very old race, with an exceedingly long history. As we know, they are parasites evolved from a kind of swamp leech. They accumulate information upon the face of crystals inside their abdomen. These crystals grow and the asutra grows. A large abdomen indicates much stored wisdom; the larger the abdomen, the higher the caste. The asutra communicate among themselves by nervous impulses, or perhaps telepathy; an array of specialised asutra is capable of the most complicated intellectual tasks.

'It is a truism that intelligence develops during a time of gradually worsening conditions; so it was with the asutra. They had and have a high reproductive rate; each asutra produces a million spawn, which are oriented according to one of two modes and which must make juncture with an opposite mode to become viable. In the early days the asutra overpopulated their swamps and were forced to compete for hosts: a challenge which urged them to domesticate hosts, to build stables and pens, and to control their own reproductive rate.

'It is important to recognise the asutra dynamic, their basic psychic drive, which is the lust to dominate a strong and active host. This necessity is as fundamental as the force which turns plants to the sunlight, or prompts men to seek food when they are hungry. Only by recognising this lust to dominate can the activities of the asutra be understood even dimly. I must remark here that many, if not all, of our original theories were naive and incorrect. My researches, I am happy to state, have illuminated the truth.

'Because of their intelligence and their capacity to multiply this intelligence, and because of their natural pedacity, asutra history has been complex and dramatic. They have passed through many eras. There was an artificial period, during which they used chemical nutrition, electrical sensations, imaginary knowledge. During a time of lassitude, mechanisms created seas of nutrient sludge, in which the asutra swam. During another era the asutra bred optimal hosts, but these were conquered and destroyed by asutra on primeval hosts from the original slime. But these archaic hosts were moribund and nearly extinct; the asutra were stimulated to interplanetary adventure.

'On the planet Kahei they discovered an environment almost identical to their own, and the Ka were compatible hosts. The asutra assumed control of Kahei, which over the centuries became to them a second home-world.

'On Kahei they encountered a most unexpected and unwelcome circumstance. By subtle degrees the Ka adapted to the asutra, and slowly the roles began to shift. The asutra, rather than being the dominant member of the symbiosis, became subordinate. The Ka began to subject the asutra to undignified uses, as control nodes for mining engines, processing machinery, and other unpleasant tasks. In other cases the Ka employed arrays of joined asutra as computing machines or reference devices; essentially the Ka used the asutra to augment their own powers, rather than the other way around. The asutra objected to such arrangements; a war occurred and the asutra on Kahei were enslaved. Henceforth the Ka were the masters and the asutra the adjuncts.

'The asutra expelled from Kahei were anxious to discover new hosts. They came to Durdane, where the human inhabitants were as agile, durable, and proficient as Ka and far more responsive to control. Durdane was too arid for their own comfort; across two or three centuries they conveyed many thousands of men and women to their home-world and integrated them into their system of life. But they still coveted the world Kahei for its idyllic moors and delightful quagmires, and therefore launched a war of annihilation against the Ka, using men as their slave warriors.

'The Ka, never a numerous folk, were assured of defeat by attrition unless they could stifle the human assault. As an experiment the Ka contrived the Roguskhoi and sent them to Durdane to destroy the human race. As we know, the experiment failed. Next the Ka thought to use men as warriors against the asutra, but again the experiment met no success; their corps of slave warriors revolted and refused to fight.'

Etzwane demanded, 'How did you learn all this?'

Ifness made a casual gesture. He had finished his soup, and was now eating a plate of assorted meats and pickled fruit. 'I employed the facilities of the Historical Institute. Dasconetta, incidentally, is discomfited; I overwhelmed his pedantic inflexibility, and indeed took the matter before Coordination, where I found active endorsement of my views. The Earth-worlds cannot tolerate human enslavement by alien races; this is fundamental policy. I accompanied the correction force in the nominal capacity of adviser to the commander, but in fact directed the expedition.

'Arriving at Kahei we found both the Ka and the asutra exhausted and discouraged with the war. In the north country we halted an engagement of warships, then enforced a peace, which was hard but fair. The Ka were required to surrender all their asutra and to repatriate all their human slaves. The asutra abandoned their attempt to dominate Kahei and also agreed to return all human hosts to Durdane. The solution to a highly complicated problem was elegantly simple, and within a common zone of comprehension. So there, in a most truncated outline, you have the situation as it exists now.' Ifness drank from a cup of verbena tea.

Etzwane sat hunched in his chair. He thought of the

silver and white ships which had driven the Ka ships back from the black asutra globes. With a pang of bitter humor he recalled how defenseless and apathetic had been the training camp, and with what illusory ease he and his men had captured it. The spaceship which they had taken with such grim determination – it actually had come to take them back to Durdane. Small wonder the resistance had been so scant!

Ifness spoke in a voice of polite concern, 'You seem troubled; has my account distressed you in any way?'

'Not at all,' said Etzwane. 'As you say, truth destroys many illusions.'

'As you can apprehend, I was preoccupied with large causes and unable to attend to the captured Alula, who presumably once again wander beside the Vurush River.' He glanced at his chronometer. 'What were your own actions subsequent to our parting?'

'They were of no great consequence,' said Etzwane. 'After some small inconvenience I returned to Shillinsk. I brought your boat back to Garwiy.'

'That is good of you. Dasconetta sent a space car down to Shillinsk for me, which of course I used.' Ifness glanced at his chronometer. 'If you will excuse me, I must leave. Our association has spanned several years, but I doubt if we will meet again. I am leaving Durdane and I do not plan to return.'

Etzwane, slumping back in his chair, said nothing. He thought of far places, of flowing rivers and nomad clans. He remembered terror aboard the transport ship and the death of Karazan; he thought of black velvet moors and the purple-black morass; he recalled Polovits and Kretzel . . . Ifness had risen to his feet. Etzwane said, 'At Shagfe is an old woman named Kretzel. She knows fourteen thousand cantos to the Great Song of the Ka. The knowledge will die with her.'

'Indeed.' Ifness hesitated, pulling at his long chin. 'I will submit this information to an appropriate agency, and Kretzel will be interviewed, no doubt to her profit. And now – '

Etzwane blurted, 'Do you require an aide, an assistant?' He had not meant to ask the question; his words had come of themselves.

Ifness smilingly shook his head. 'Such an association would surely be impractical. Gastel Etzwane: goodbye.' He departed the inn.

Etzwane sat still and alone for fifteen minutes. Then he rose and went to another table across the room. His appetite had vanished; he called for a flask of strong wine. He became aware of music: Frolitz and the Pink-Black-Azure-Deep Greeners played a pleasant air of the Lor-Asphen uplands.

Frolitz came to stand by the table. He laid a hand on Etzwane's shoulder. 'The man is gone, and just as well. He has had a baneful influence upon you; in fact he has distracted you from your music. Now he is gone, and things will be as before. Come play your khitane.'

Etzwane looked into the depths of the cool wine, studying the lights and colors. 'He is gone, but tonight I have no stomach for music.'

'Stomach?' scoffed Frolitz. 'Who plays with his stomach? We use hands and breath and merry inclinations.'

'True. But my fingers are numb; I would embarrass us all. Tonight I will sit and listen, and drink a glass or two of wine, and tomorrow we will decide.' He looked towards the door, though he knew that Ifness had gone.

THE ANOME

Jack Vance

Durdane Book

A world of strange ways and stranger people. A land where men and women are marked for life. Where they are bound to irrevocable destinies by the proclamations of the Faceless Man – an unseen power which terrorises and controls the world.

Durdane is a place where defiance is punished with death. But this kingdom of myriad mystery and incalculable peril is now threatened by a menace from without – the dreaded Rogushkoi. And only one youth, Gastel Etzwane, dares to challenge the unchallengeable, the power of the Faceless Man, in an extraordinary struggle for mastery and for the survival of Durdane . . .

CORONET BOOKS

THE BRAVE FREE MEN

Jack Vance

Durdane Book 2

The Faceless Man is a prisoner in his own palace. His power over the people of Durdane is in the hands of Gastel Etzwane, a youth whose thirst for vengeance against the dreaded Rogushkoi would be slaked only by oceans of their blood. For these invincible foes who threatened Durdane had taken and killed his mother and sister.

To destroy the Rogushkoi Gastel would have to unite a world that survived only through its separateness. It was more than dangerous, but he had no choice. If they were to fight the people must regain control of their own lives. Only then could Gastel recruit an elite corps of the liberated – the Brave Free Men – to fling against the Rogushkoi and fight to the death . . .

CORONET BOOKS

THE EXPENDABLES: THE DEATHWORMS OF KRATOS

Richard Avery

They were THE EXPENDABLES – some genuine volunteers, others not. They were the chosen ones – the people who had been 'selected' to travel far into space and find new planets for human colonisation.

KRATOS was the first planet of call, inhabited by gigantic creatures that swayed and roared, that were blessed with seven eyes and mouths cavernous enough to suck in a handful of humans at a time.

And KRATOS is only the first locale in a glittering new series of books that will wrench you into the most terrifying of unknown worlds . . .

CORONET BOOKS